BY THE SAME AUTHOR

*The Hosanna Man*
*Common People*
*Native Ground*
*A Pledge for the Earth*
*The Honeymooners*
(*play*)
*Turning Point*
*Clipped Wings*
*The Real Life*
*In My Own Land*
*Going to the Moon*
*The Bliss Body*
*The Lamb*
(*radio play*)

# FLESH OF MORNING

PHILIP CALLOW
# Flesh of Morning

THE BODLEY HEAD
LONDON SYDNEY
TORONTO

With thanks to The Arts Council for financial assistance during the writing of this novel.

*Flesh of Morning* is the final volume in a trilogy. The first two volumes are *Going to the Moon* and *The Bliss Body*.

© Philip Callow 1971
ISBN 0 370 01452 9
Printed and bound in Great Britain for
The Bodley Head Ltd
9 Bow Street, London WC2E 7AL
by Cox & Wyman Ltd, Fakenham
Set in Monotype Imprint
*First published 1971*

To Christian

# I

WHY IT happens I don't know, but every so often I want to go swinging back, link up with childhood again. Live it again, taste it, walk in that light. Not that it was all light, Christ no—but the issues were so much clearer. It's as if there's a vital clue to the present misery I need to find, I've lost it somewhere, so I go combing through the succulent young grass, the pure snow, sifting and searching. Was misery inside or outside then? Did it come seeping out of the bricks, the ground, leaking down from the sky—or am I reversing the flow? I'm asking, is it me or them? Is the world a poisoned and tragic place now, so that the only hope or virtue is in being nimble enough to sidestep the fall-out, tucked away in some uncontaminated spot, no radios, no papers, head down and the fog billowing over? I'd be a liar though if I gave the impression that every swing back into the past was a deliberate attempt to find out how this stone wedged in my chest came to be stuck there. That's daft: life's not a bloody detective story. Going back is pure instinct with me: begin at the beginning.

That time when I was ten or eleven and I had my brother with me, we took a small ridge tent, just big enough to lie down in side by side if you kept your arms straight, and we had sandwiches and fat bottles of coloured pop, rolled groundsheet, all distributed carefully in the two haversacks slung on our backs. The instant I got mine on I felt grave, responsible, older. Off we went stoutly to catch the bus, mother waving on the doorstep. I had the most to carry, being the elder.

'Watch the traffic, Colin! Look after him!'

She waved us out of sight, dwindling pathetically, and this always undermined me at the outset, looking back as we turned the corner. Goodbye! We could have been crossing continents, entering jungles, instead of tramping down to the bus station for the 28 to the boundary. It must have been my idea to go in a field not far from the aerodrome, and what made it momentous was the thought of staying the night—we'd got permission, we could if we wanted. It was August, dry, windless: the foliage had run riot and exhausted itself, huge dusty nettles in the ditches, dock leaves, the summer bolted and gone to seed. It all hung there, that was the feeling.

You got off the bus and walked for a few minutes, went over a little hump-backed bridge and there was the field to the right, where we'd been with our mother and father once on a picnic. The ground was rough, a wilderness of spiky thistles, tall thick-stemmed brutes, and so many nettle beds you had to pick your way like a goat. It was worse than I'd remembered, so bad that I began to wonder if we'd gone wrong somehow—and then I saw the dried-up stream choked with big jagged stones, the baked mud full of hoof-holes where the cows had trampled down the low bank for a watering place. This was the spot alright, only now it was changed subtly: no parents, no protection, now everything bristled, looked hostile. My brother stumbled, twisted his foot in a rut and whimpered. When I glanced at him he looked away.

The very silence frightened me, and the strange air of desertion. I hated it, the field was ugly in a malignant, menacing sort of way, I wanted to run off home. What was happening? Without speaking we unpacked the tent and started to put it up: it was so small the steel pegs were like meat skewers, you just shoved them into the ground with the heel of your hand. But it hurt, the earth was iron-hard: one after another the skewers bent. More antagonism—the field didn't want us, I felt. Biting my lip I went searching for a softer spot, the blackness congealing in me, while overhead the sky was clouding and lowering like a lid, all without a breeze, and in absolute silence.

'What's up, Alan?'
'Nothing.'
'Foot hurt?'
'Didn't hurt me foot.'
'What was it, then?'
'Ankle.'
'Alright, is it?'
'Suppose so.'

We pitched camp again, desperate now, made our hands sore getting the skewers in, spread out the groundsheet as if we were really staying, but I knew we weren't. I was the elder, I had to bluff it out. We sat nervously in the mouth of our tent, doorflaps rolled back and tied with the tapes and inside that snug, womb-like look a small tent has, the yellow filtered light on the smooth groundsheet with its rubber smell, sleeping-bag laid out—it really looked inviting. I sat there hugging my knees, munching the soggy tomato sandwiches and guzzling the fizzy strawberry pop—I couldn't wait to get away from there. The weather was my excuse; not that Alan cared. He was scared too, I could sense it, either by the silence or the field itself, the ugly look of it: or he might have caught the feeling from me. What had I caught it from? I didn't stop to ask, it was such a relief going.

In a way it was like a sudden attack of homesickness, very treacherous: like going away on a camp with the scouts for that first time. Devon, a lush creamy landscape opening and folding, all its flesh overripe, steep ferny hills, marching up the green rooted lanes sniffing waves of fragrance, and suddenly out on the crest of an amazing new world, the sky hitting you in a great stroke of surprise, the sea far below shivering like an animal—and the light. The clean sea air inside your shirt, up your legs. To be tipped off the lorry with all the tents and equipment into a world like that, lying in the dim bell tent, feet to the pole, and all you could do was ache for the dirty scabby street where your mother lived and nothing else, blind and deaf to it all, your whole being tuned to one far-off point of departure . . . And what a labour camp they made it, our beloved leaders. Up at six digging latrines, getting breakfast, running cross-country races, while the senior scouts and rovers lolled on the grass drawling out orders, sunburnt and handsome giants with their fat thighs and hairy forearms. They lorded it all the week, joking among themselves, very conscious of being an elite. And no resentment from us, not a crumb—it was the same old pattern of school and home we were used to: anyway we were too young to question anything. At night we bought chocolate and slabs of toffee from the tuck shop and lay in bed chewing till we were sick, and I never stopped longing for home, every waking second, all the fibres of my body.

## 2

THEY SAY, oh I didn't know you wrote things, and immediately you feel wrong, disgusted. For all kinds of reasons and nonreasons. Number one: they haven't read anything and they're not going to, even now—the important thing for them is that it's printed and you get money for it. Money spells importance. All the shit that gets printed daily, surely they can see there's no honour in the mere achievement of print. I want to tell them, you wouldn't have come up glowing to know me when the stuff I was writing wasn't being printed . . . and then I think, how stupid, they wouldn't even have known of its existence: I made sure of that. Not even my brother, my mother and father. There is the same instinct now, maybe even stronger today, to disown the art that comes out of me. Something is not quite right about it, and buried deep in a drawer it doesn't matter, but when it's out and read and the tiny accumulations of comment testify to its existence, then that's terrible. You want to howl at them to shut up because they're ignorant of the reasons, there are reasons they'll never know about. Can't they tell that?

Art needs to be handled gingerly, it isn't safe. Artists are liars. Better to be just a national insurance number. I'd rather dig holes in the road, it's more honourable. Always this finger itch to make a pattern, to order the chaos, find out why. Going up to Nottingham, no job, nowhere to live, just to be near Leila and continue the agony. Why? Because of the chaos, and the ice age we're in, swarming millions walled in, roads everywhere and no directions, and in spite of that a woman could warm you up with a flick of her eyelashes, could touch you with her voice in a way that made you tender about the clothes she wore, the rooms and gardens and streets and weather she moved through to reach you. Regal, fateful, powerfully coming. Sure as fate. I wanted more of that. I had just discovered what it meant to be intimate with a woman. Trust me to pick one who didn't belong to me, who liked me alright but only wanted me for an affair. What's an affair? Well, I'm jumping over great gobbets of misery, no end of twists and turns before I finally manage one night to box her into a corner and make her cry. How women loathe to face facts when it doesn't suit, how direct they are with them when it does. So she stopped fencing at last one night and said, calm as you like: 'I love my husband.' Or words to that effect.

'Oh good,' I said bitterly. 'Where does that leave us?'

'Colin, it doesn't make the slightest difference,' she said, smiling. I stared amazed, eyes burning back into my head. I really thought I was mad at last.

'It doesn't?'

'No, of course not.'

'Sorry, I'm lost.'

'I love you both, in different ways,' she said, perfectly serious.

'Do you really?' I could hear myself saying, eking it out. Punishment was all I could give. I got ready.

'Yes. I mean it, Colin.'

'Christ yes, I'm sure you do. How bloody convenient.'

She took it, I hunted over her face for signs of anger, hurt. Nothing. For the first time I was humiliated, but the despair kept talking.

'I'm lost,' I said.

Loving her to excess had sapped my strength. Now I was weak and dangerous. And this was the beginning of the end. But we kept on, grimly. Then the amazing thing happened, the meeting with Aline, with absolutely no effort or act of will on my part, the first time it's ever happened like this.

Go back a bit: that meeting is too important, crucial, I mustn't rush at it. Go back to the hallucinatory few months in the cottage in Devon with Ray and Connie, one night of delirium in Leicester and then the collapse, the fever. On with the grind again, though instead of the screaming factory I'd found a builders' merchants in the city and was a warehouse clerk. A pricing clerk, they called me. Strangest, most demoralising job I've ever had. I was there four weeks and at the end of it I still didn't know what I was supposed to do, except look busy. Why they took me on in the first place I'll never know. Nobody spoke to me by name, I went in and out of that dump like a ghost. Yet it was interesting, if you could summon up enough detachment—an Aladdin's cave on several floors, stacked to the roof with bins of nails, cleats, ragbolts, racks of S-bends, gutters, lavatory pans, and for dozens of items they seemed to have a secret language. Only I was too young for detachment. Also I was obsessed by time, and in this place it dragged terribly. If I could have wandered about exploring, peering in all the musty corners, it wouldn't have been bad, but I was supposed to be pinned at my desk fluttering papers, doing nothing and looking busy. I had a few bills in front of me, to work out the prices—eight bags at fourteen and sixpence—and there were half a dozen items on each bit of flimsy paper and the whole lot took me about twenty minutes, dragging it out. I asked for some work once, really desperate. The chief clerk looked at me as if I'd said some dirty word or left my flies open—I swore to myself I'd grow roots before I asked again.

Even in those days—especially then—it came as no surprise to me, the situation. I'd suspected for a long time that for all its apparent order and efficiency the world was definitely unhinged in some basic, never-to-be-admitted way. You had to humour the bastards, that was the game. Because they were the ones who doled out the bread and butter. So here I was stuck in this long slit of an office, windows so small and high that you couldn't have seen out even if the muck had been scraped off them, here I sat picking my nose day after day and getting paid for it and it didn't strike me as at all peculiar. Just the way of the world. It was stupid to get angry but I did sometimes, seized up with rage suddenly for no reason, which made me lurch to my feet and go slithering out to the lavatory, a prison cell down on the next floor with the usual window too high. At least it was private, with the bolt across you could just stand there like a bloody stork and go into a trance. That was a great luxury, not having to look busy. Worth a ten-bob rise, that. And by standing on the wobbly seat you could see a corner of the building opposite, another warehouse, a bit of the wavy asbestos roof, a scrap of sky. Funny how you felt the need to convince yourself that there was an outside. Amazing how attractive it looked, even the few scraps you could catch sight of—how it beckoned, seduced you: the sounds of kids playing, rag-and-bone man howling like a wolf, women's voices. They drifted up and your eardrums would snatch at them, suck them in of their own accord. You got a thrill then because the walls melted, you were out, liberated, in those few seconds as the sounds hung there in your head.

Nothing on the walls to read. I wrote letters to Leila in there, and to my mother. Ray was still with me in the cottage: nobody else to write to. The amazing simplicity of my life, so uncluttered and so pointless. That was what the seizure of rage meant—I see now. The job fitted me like a glove, it expressed me perfectly. Then it wasn't possible to do anything except react, pour out the love-letters spiced with sex and longing, topped with poetic sauce, own brand. Say good morning, evening.

# 3

ONE DAY the chief clerk lifted his head and I finally became aware that he was staring at me. This is it, I thought, cards. The bullet. And for some insane reason felt guilty. Still staring, horn rims glinting, greasy black hair glued flat on his skull, parted dead centre as if by a knife. A sharp, short-arsed Liverpool lad, promoted and shipped down by Head Office, so the locals hated him: the new broom, there to streamline the system and galvanise the sleepy south. Now it was my turn.

'A moment?' he was saying. To me. No, he wasn't being sarcastic, he actually meant it.

I stood there. He had a bundle of papers for me.

'We'll put you on checking,' he said, hands ferreting, eyes down. They nearly all have this insulting habit of not looking, when they get you there. 'See Jim Foster,' I heard, so I shoved off.

Jim was a fatherly Devonian, he grunted like a bear but was amiable enough, even on Mondays. He was a family man: written all over him. He plodded, conducted a choir; sometimes his left leg hurt, a legacy of the war. Then his big round body moved a bit irritably and once he swore softly, only once, being a churchman. I looked at him, interested, hopeful, but he was sunk deep in his family fat, impregnable, no winkling him out. What happened on the surface was incidental. I sat next to him every day for the last week I was there while he patiently sorted out little problems for me and I knew he was wasting his time. I wasn't staying. Any day now.

He'd been in the army, Libya, Tripoli, Tobruk, Alamein.

Got wounded and taken prisoner in '42. 'Lovely job that was. Lucky to be out of it.'

Soon he would have clocked up twelve years of service with this firm. I reckoned up. 'You came here straight from school then, did you, before the war?'

'That's it, me 'andsome.'

'Twelve years, in this one room?'

'You've got it, me lover.'

Queer that he never got curious about me, I thought, marvelling at this matter-of-factness, his warm muddy nature which oozed placidly like his body. Then once a prickle of awareness told me that he was mildly curious at last, even before he hauled up the words:

'You aren't from down here, lad.' Speculating, you could hardly call it questioning.

'No, Black Country.'

'Up the line, eh.'

'Straight up till you get to the Bull Ring,' I said and grinned, seeing the same single-line track to the north whenever they trotted out this phrase.

Things livened up momentarily when the reps breezed in on Friday mornings, the room filling up, suddenly taken over by expansive, blustery back-slappers, freebooters flaunting it in front of the desk-chained clerks, lighting up the room with jaunty talk, broad smiles. Some with beer guts, belly laughs, some thin scrannels, one dark Irishman with burning eyes, Red Indian cheekbones, but most of the eyes were shrewd and dead, shamelessly worming straight in. All the same I liked the reckless air that came wafting in at the door on Friday, heralding the weekend. I liked to hear the door bang open, no respect, with Liverpool glaring through his goggles and being ignored: they had no time for him.

'What d'ja know, Jim, old cock?' a man they called Smithy would shout—he was the loudest.

'Not much, or I wouldn't be here,' was the stock answer.

Hearing this bovine character say it made me raise my eyebrows: somehow it was too flip, too cynical, as if he was trying to imitate the tone of the reps.

They were from the outside, so it gave them a shoddy glamour. The freedom of the road came in with them, and it disturbed me for the rest of the day. I felt effervescent, I sighed like a lover, I sat there with ears flapping for news of the outer world. Listening, I was doubly sure. I was on the road out. I sat mouselike and checked and cross-checked, next to a bear who grunted and rubbed his gammy leg, who didn't know much or he wouldn't be there. Drank my tea— one sugar please.

Got to dinnertime and I'd be out, rain or shine, roaming the backstreets, aimless, stretching my legs, sucking down air and liberation, then because the freedom was sandwiched between bouts of prison it was soon a mockery and a burden, a dreary killing of time. What time is it? As a kid out walking with my brother we used to ask old men with watch-chains showing on their stomachs 'Have you got the right time please?' just for the pleasure of it, and to see who guessed the nearest. I still didn't have a watch. Had one once in my teens, when I was a bit of a fop with a flash strap of expanding chrome steel. Felt strangled: couldn't bear one on my wrist. Hated the symbolism, the insanity of minutes, seconds, life chopped up and regulated like that, tripping down the drain with a goosestep rhythm. So I was always looking for clocks on high buildings, peering into the interiors of shops and getting queer looks from shop assistants, asking passers-by.

Out at dinnertimes into a sleazy district, a clutter of backstreets, a rag-tag of roofs and chimneys, bolted on like a rusty grid to Union Street, famed for its herds of sailors of all nationalities, aiming them straight and true for the Halfpenny Bridge, the sailors' barracks, Aggie Weston's, the Salvation Army and the docks. Or the town if you were going the other road. Once famous for drunken fights, coppers prowling in pairs, now it was tame and just dirty, bashed about by the war and the stuffing littered everywhere. Gaping holes, piles of rubble, valerian sprouting from the mortar, fireplaces rusting out in mid-air. Buildings going up here and there, behind the corrugated palisades. It was winter, pinched, often raining and blowing. The windy city. I moochchd about with my collar up, sometimes with a pasty stuck in my fist like one of the regulars. Out from Tavy Cottages into the Octagon, along by the gents' outfitters—short and tall, we fit them all—and the barber's, pub, tobacconist, a brewery, and cross over to look at the pulp magazines. That meat. Junk shops, taxi office with a scuffed counter and some weary-looking fireside chairs, all different: man behind the counter grinning out vacantly with every tooth in his head. A tattoo artist. Stand and gaze at the fly-blown photos, most of them known by heart. Elderly man with thin white arms embroidered thickly from wrist to armpit, a dragon billowing up from his belly-button. The skin of his body corpse-white. Women with bone-poor faces and childish eyes, smiling, naked but clothed in intricate design from head to toe. A young woman with a face case-hardened by experience like a pro, stripped to the waist and bloodless like the others, full breasts decorated in flower petals round each nipple.

Down Battery Street to Peel Street, past the chaotic little shop filled to the ceiling with bikes and lumps of machinery for the breakers, the notice still in the window with the comic spelling: 'Wanted, Washing machines, dryers, iol heaters, hand sewing machines, radios, friges, vacuums, ions. Enquireries, 37 Alma Street West.' Felt the destitution like a curse.

Find myself one day outside the big ornamental gates of the naval hospital. Bottle-green ironwork towering up, the coat of arms, anchors, tridents freshly gilded, and not far inside I can see a rack of punch cards and a clock, the commissionaire's box, the flower beds and the cushions of turf, lime trees, and planted in the middle of the grass a white-painted ship's mast with rigging, rope ladder and crow's nest, where they must run up the damn flag or whatever they do. I stared in through the railings like an urchin. Read the notice in the glass-fronted box about visiting times to all wards 'with the exception of Zymotics Ward'. Signed by the surgeon admiral. Going away, following the long stone wall back to the granite warehouse and my chair, desk, papers, I kept telling myself to remember that word 'zymotic', God knows why. The very sight of it up there on a public board struck me as fantastic, and them expecting you to know. Well, you might, if your friend or relative was one. A zymotic! More likely I wanted to remember it for Ray, to try it out on him. If the mood was right. You had to be in the mood for a word like that.

The men of no fixed abode I used to see in the streets, hanging round the steps of the church hostel in King Street, by the scaly old railway arches running with slime and dog piss: derelicts, crazy buggers, homeless old men. I used to admire them, underdogs and outcasts, they were free, they weren't in the clutches sitting stupid in a sunless room all day, they were out in the weather. Wanderers. I didn't want to see how they were chained to the gutters, noses rubbed in the stink of dustbins. Youth grabs what it needs and bounces away, marvellously elastic. Now and then I'd see a city tramp they called Claude, short, shambling, thing like a baseball cap rammed on his skull. Under the peak his charred face screwed up in a permanent ferocious squint. Shirt open to the waist, winter and summer. If he wasn't foraging in a litter bin, arm plunged in right to the armpit, he'd be swaying on the edge of the kerb spewing obscenities at the traffic. 'Fuckin' bastids, bastids!' he screamed. Never saw him without his potato sack slung over his back like an unspeakable Santa Claus. At the newsagents he read the racing results from a paper in one of the wire racks outside, lifting up the corner with one hand and aiming his squint through a magnifying glass held in the other. Once he was straightening up from a bin with a squashed tomato he'd rescued—an old lady said 'here' and held out a bun to him, as you would offer one to an elephant in the zoo: not too close because of the stink, the strangeness. He sent it flying with one swipe and swore at her.

What about the poor bastard they said was a shellshock case – twice he nearly gave me a heart attack. He had a habit of breaking into a wild gallop, leaping in the air and letting out a loud hiss between his teeth like a blown pressure valve, all at the same time. And he had one of these mad fits as he came level with me under the railway bridge, coming up from behind. My shoulders twitched up, my guts wrenched, heart gave a sickening lurch. Twice he caught me like that. Tall, gangling, a lopsided face with a coconut tuft of gingery hair, expression like a frightened schoolboy. As if terrified of himself, what he might do next. 'Isn't it dreadful,' you heard ladies murmur. 'He has a wife and family, you know, oh yes, lovely woman, she won't live with him any more. Wouldn't you think somebody could do something?'

Going past a gutted shop, only the front walls and a broken window frame left, I saw the sign on the square of red tin poking out in the street like a railway signal: Drink Vimto. Took me back in a rush to pre-war, to those summery evenings around Harbourne. I sat meekly in the back of the big Siddley my uncle drove for his firm, my aunt beside him, queening it, and in the back with me wallowing in the brown leather was my cousin Margaret. Well away in her corner, plenty of space between us—I was the poor relation. That didn't matter, I wasn't bothered: not then. It all went with the car, the sumptuous walnut dashboard, my uncle's elbow out of the offside window and the panache of his driving, strumming on his knee with his left hand. Early as that, young as I was, I knew the smell of power and money, the assurance that went with it, the swank and ignorance and fish-eyed patronage. Nobody heeded the vast pure power of the sky and the stillness that belonged to that, the day running out calmly, trickling away like the last of the tide, leaving this enormous peaceful feeling in the wash of sunlight. The land glowing beyond the hedges in flakes of gold, scorching a wood. The leaves smouldered, went out. We went wafting on rich springs through the lanes frothing to the rims with pale umbels of cowparsley, hemlock, angelica, with elders, hazels, stirring the verges and making the cows stare. Suddenly Margaret yelled out, 'Stop the car, daddy, I want a Vimto!'

Not please or can we stop. I could have seen my father stopping. We swung in at the Red Lion, pulled up with sedate majesty in a crunch of gravel and as my uncle climbed out he said over his shoulder, 'What does Colin want?' When she didn't answer he said a little peevishly, 'Margaret?'

'How should I know?' she screeched. I was used to these situations, but I still squirmed. They went with the car. My uncle was alright, I could get on with him fine when we were alone, it was the family man side I couldn't stand: the three of them together. This was the man who stuck his face in the window and said, wagging his sleek head, widening his watery eyes, 'Will my family and nephew for Christ's sake tell me what I am required to fetch from this hostelry?' Which was nothing much, but the tone was poisonous.

I'd have one of those fruit drinks, dark and sugary, the Vimto thing, sucking it up through the straw and holding down the belches. My uncle drank his beer with a big facial performance, lip-smacking noises, ahs and ums, and then he belched. 'Jack!' his wife said, from force of habit, or it might have been for my benefit. Margaret cuddled into the corner with her bottle: she was my age but she liked to act babyish. She was soft-looking, a girl. She smelled different. Strange. I wanted to poke my finger in her flesh, to feel the difference.

# 4

GIRLS. I went to see the girl from Leeds, the art student who was working at Butlins for the summer. She had a vacation job. Pwllheli. Looked on the map to find it, up and down the Welsh bulge—ah yes. Over twenty-one and still hadn't met a girl I could talk to, be with. Christ, you had to be desperate to go to Pwllheli, wherever it was, just to meet a girl. I was desperate in a quiet way and I had the photo to go on—dark hair, eyes, uptilted face looking a little arrogant for the camera—and the letters were friendly, though I had to admit, cool. Hell, what would I be doing all holiday anyway except mooning about the house, going for melancholy walks to the edge of the streets and across a stile into the meadows on warm evenings, taking a book, say Rimbaud—'melancholy golden wash of the setting sun'. Look on the map and find Pwllheli, trace the route. Send a note and then go before she had a chance to say no—nothing to lose. Meet her, see what happens. The will and the desperation forcing to create meetings, against the hermit instinct and the gag of shyness. The will won the first round, always, then drawing nearer the awful conflict fought itself out in my guts. White and sick and sweating, vowing never again. But I get there. The fear of failure worse than the dread of disgrace.

My mother showed remarkable restraint whenever I said I was going here or there. Strange journeys, visits, with no reasons ever offered: surely she must have been dying to know. She didn't ask. Wouldn't. I was grateful, but it was unnerving and in the end left me more guilty than a row and recriminations would have done, because this way there was no opportunity for anger. I couldn't rage righteously when they refused to pry, couldn't rebel against the stupid restrictions and narrow minds. No opposition, nothing. A clear road. Well, I knew that was a lie, but I kept quiet and just hopped it. Held my face straight and said, casual as you like:

'Going to North Wales for a few days. Wander round a bit.'

'All right. You'll need some clean underwear—when were you thinking of going?'

'Oh, Monday I think.'

As soon as she became concerned over anything, she frowned like a girl.

Afterwards I thought, the letter postmarked Pwllheli which came. She's not a fool, my mother: though I doubt if she'd ever heard of the place. It wasn't that, it was just her knack for putting two and two together.

The train journey was dreamlike, now I think of it. I went across from the Midlands, changed somewhere and was blind to everything, so preoccupied with the struggle inside. All inner attention, like a man near to being mad. The only thing I noticed was that the Pwllheli place was as far as the train went: terminus. First time I'd seen a railway track ending at a pair of buffers inside the station, except for London. It made the whole thing so ridiculously portentous, me getting off at the end of the line carrying a handful of things in a weekend bag—like a bad film. But the station almost cheered me up, light and airy and clean, small, lots of painted wood, sun shining gaily through the glass skylights, and going through the ticket barrier to a completely new town. It began to feel good to be lost.

I walked about for an hour getting the feel of the town, wondering vaguely where the sea was, not caring a damn about it, still dominated by the stifled tug-of-war in my chest, the endless warfare I kept trying to blot out by a refrain that went roughly like this: if anything happens it happens, if it doesn't it doesn't—what have I got to lose? Jesus, here I was nearly falling off the end of the peninsula and they'd got a Woolworth's, a seasidy, country one, bare clattering board floor and antiquated counters. And bang opposite was the Co-op. Stone buildings, short twisty streets, nothing much to it but for the moment I couldn't sort out the pattern. Suddenly I felt drained, dragged out by the strain and strangeness. I went in like a dreamwalker through the glass front of a café and sat drinking tea, eating a piece of sawdust cake—jukebox playing 'Put another nickel in . . .' A gang of kids, youths and girls, tumbled in and started fooling about, letting out self-conscious squawks and giggles that set my teeth on edge, drawing attention to things I thought I'd accepted, the bubbly bleak music, stamped-out plastic cups and saucers, candy-floss pink walls and lollipop people. But it was the plate glass I really loathed. I sat by the glass wall and I could see out, only I wasn't out. A lie. A trick. As if it didn't matter whether you were in or out of the horrible bloody dump. Soon we won't know the difference, it'll be painless. I got up and went out, saw a sign that said 'To the seafront' and started walking that way in a trance, looking in front windows of houses for a bed and breakfast sign. Soon found a trim little terraced house and was going up the doll's house staircase inside to approve the room.

'That's very nice,' nodding.
'When would you like your breakfast?' the woman said.
'What time?'
'I don't mind.'
'Eight, is that too early for you?'
'Oh no.'
'I'll give you a call, shall I?'

In the soft fussy room I lay still, smelling camphor, staring up at the plank ceiling, the nails, the joints, telling myself that this was Wales, a morning in Wales. Nothing seemed much different: I always expect dramatic differences. The woman's singsong was hardly noticeable but she had to bring hot water in a tall white jug and leave it outside the door. I heard it then, Wales.

'You'll see the washbasin,' she called. 'Young man?'

'Yes, thank you very much.'

When I opened the door for the jug I could smell the bacon, even hear the busy sizzle. I was hungry, I was here, I'd nearly done it. My spirits began to lift, the mere fact of being here rejuvenated me. Life was easy if you just let it happen. I was cocky now. I poured the hot water into the basin, touched it with my finger. Too hot. Then I spotted another, even bigger jug, a tin one, under the marble-topped washstand. Cold water. Life was simple, hot and cold, one problem at a time.

Found the post office and bought a letter card: sat on a bench, a warm sunless morning, and wrote to her. Dear Julie, I'm here, when can you meet me and where? Just say the time and the place—don't work too hard. Probably nothing like that but it was brief. I hadn't got into my stride writing letters to her from home. Had to meet her first, I kept telling myself, but something in me sank like a stone at the thought. Those replies of hers, they were so bloody dead. And ominous. What the hell, who cares about letters, I don't want a pen friend, I want a girl. Flesh and bones and blood. And so on. Inside I was far from hopeful.

That afternoon I went into a stationer's and there was a table of books for sale, remainders, paper jackets soiled. Walked out with one called 'Why Abstract' and followed the sign to the coast, meaning to sit on a bench and read my book. Went by a large guest-house on the corner, black-and-white painted windows, stranded between the sea and the town, and then there was nothing, nobody. The road curved to the right beside the sand dunes, full of purpose, then it ran on blankly. I sat on a rock and stared at the sea, watched a seagull which happened to be directly ahead, offering itself to the horizon, and for the life of me I couldn't bring myself to move my head one way or the other, it was such a desolate-looking coast, such a Godforsaken spot. Like sitting at the edge of the world. It was warm in town, but not here. The breeze had a bite in it, the whole feel of the place was abrasive, cold, inhospitable. I was beyond feeling a repulsion for it: just frozen. Got up and turned my back, walked almost eagerly towards the town, the knot of streets, shoppers and loungers, the holidaymakers gawping, scribbling their postcards, hunting down gifts. I went and sat in the snack bar again. Wales for the Welsh. Dear Julie, hurry up and I hope to Christ you've got a friendly face. Collecting my egg and chips I even smiled wanly at the girl behind the counter, one human being to another. Not a flicker. Deep freeze handmaiden.

Julie turned out to be the same, expressionless. I met her at seven, after her day at Butlins—perhaps that was the trouble. And she could have been bodiless as we went up the same blank road to that wind-scraped coast and I gazed ahead fixedly, numb with the cold, the icy aura of her, and struggled to wring out words, make contact, when the truth was I couldn't wait to get away, none of it meant a thing, we were wasting our time.

She was making me more and more insipid; I hated her for that.

'Had a hard day?'
'Oh, so-so.'
'How long will you be here?'
'Another three weeks yet.'
Halted, crossed over, walked on, burdened by defeat.
'Like it here?'
'What's that?'
'This place, do you like it?'
'Not much.'

She looked neat and unruffled in her cornflower blue, but her indifference was showing. She wasn't amused by my persistence, she wasn't anything.

'You the only student?'
'Where, at the camp?'
'The camp, yes.'
'Oh no, there are six or seven. At least. Two French boys. They're nice.'

That's how it went.

# 5

IT WAS more or less the same fiasco with Connie's friend Jan when she came for a holiday that time: it must have been Easter. I was in the cottage with Ray and Connie and the baby, sharing—first of all sleeping on a camp bed in the living room because there was only one bedroom, then a couple in the village let me have a bedroom for a pound a week, and that was better, we could spread out a bit. Fact was, the good life we'd embraced so innocently had begun to crumble. Our jobs had undermined it, Ray's and mine, and in the evenings I was stuck there night after night, too tired to move out, blocking their marriage with dreams of adultery. The woman up the line, beckoning, intriguing. I might even have been writing a letter to her when Connie suddenly sang out: 'Hey folks, listen to this – Jan's coming!'

Ray lifted his head, startled. 'How d'you mean? A holiday?'

'Of course,' Connie crowed, 'what did you think I meant?'

'Isn't she working then?'

Connie gave one of her big yells of laughter; she was really zooming about inside with her news. 'It's Easter next week, daftie!'

And naturally Connie was bound to feel gay: for weeks Ray and me had been going in to work together, sometimes meeting on the way home and anyway swopping talk and ideas at night, jawing on about books, writing fan letters to one or two writers and speculating endlessly on their lives, struggles, developments. Utterly dreamy, ridiculous, up-in-the-clouds thoughts, the kind of idealistic boyish unworldly guff that women hear mostly in silence, sitting in a corner. When they get their heads together it's for something much more personal. Either that or gossip. It has to be of some concern to them, to affect them personally.

So Jan was coming. This would even things up for her. I imagine too that she thought things might end with me fixed up with a girl friend—let's say at least that the thought crossed her mind—and then I'd be off their necks for a while, thank God. Who could blame anyone for hoping? Only it wasn't to be. I hadn't met Jan, so naturally I was curious, and the night before she was due we decided to make the room festive and tack up the watercolours we'd done that winter. We had a pile of daubs between us—up they went all round the fireplace, the window, even on the door. Seeing the brave show, nipping outside to peer in at the window at night just to observe the effect, a cave of colour, a jewel box (like that flash of glory in the glimpse of Gauguin's hut at the close of *Moon and Sixpence*—or did I dream it?)—it looked so inviting, token of the good life we'd nearly talked away down the drain, that I began to wish I wasn't leaving after all. I'd more or less decided, secretly, to go straight after Easter.

When I say the same fiasco I don't mean that Jan was in the least like Julie. On the contrary, they couldn't have differed more, those two. Julie the typical self-conscious teenager, knowing, face gummed up none too artistically with make-up, and under it the frozen virgin. Sealed and waiting for the one and only, the man she would marry. He would unlock her, no one else. But Jan's effect on me was equally disastrous, simply because she was vulnerable, shrinking almost visibly from further hurt, and for me that made her virtually untouchable. I couldn't bear to be the one, her awareness filled me with anguish, I shrank back instinctively from the responsibility. Not me. Yet how tender she was with the baby, silently bending over, and sensitive in her listening to people, withdrawn and yet you felt she was registering nuances, tones, her small intense face had that kind of quick snatching intelligence. She could be a bitch too, I was sure, from one or two stinging answers she gave—though as a rule she sat quiet. Cramped up in silence. You longed to say the word that would unlock her, make her life pour, and ended up horribly afflicted instead with the same disease if you had any tendencies that way yourself, as I did. She was contagious. I was afraid of her. Her silences were glutinous, they made me feel sick. She was the last thing I wanted. Tall, awkward, large-boned, a tortured Yorkshire girl. I went one night into town with her to see a film, it was *Mr Deeds*, on at the Scala, one of those enormous baroque picture palaces they used to build in the thirties, heyday of the cinema, gilt and velvet and plush everywhere, a scarlet and gold heaven to keep the workers happy in their back-to-backs, enough room in there to seat a thousand. Off we went to catch the bus and there was Connie in the hall making sheep's eyes at us, chortling over our 'date'.

'Hurry up, you'll be late,' she hooted, looking meaningfully, private-public, at Ray, who was doing his best to stay non-committal.

'I was born late,' I said.

'Keep your hair on, we're going,' Jan said, flinty-eyed. They'd worked together in the same office somewhere, once upon a time. Bits of old slang and familiarity kept popping out. They enjoyed this. They had their own relationship, connected with this, which they liked to revive and renew every so often with the old language. And their own brand of humour. This way they could assert themselves, escape from Ray and me if they wanted, thumbing their noses in the process. We couldn't follow into those thickets, or at least I couldn't, I didn't know any of the code.

The film we'd chosen to see couldn't have been a more ironic choice, for in it shyness was enshrined as a virtue, as the most paramount shining thing. All the way through it was integrity and lump in the throat and fumbling, butterfingered innocence in the midst of corruption, a triumph of the ordinary speechless man who has his values straight, who recites bits of poems on doorsteps, then falls over the dustbin in confusion, love and confusion. That sounds like sarcasm, but at the time I loved it and the Gary Cooper hero passionately, in fact for years after. Went to see every film he appeared in, though I never experienced that kind of thrill again. It was fantasy of course—shyness cripples, it never triumphs—but how it encouraged and pampered me, gave me a super-ego to live up to, made me glamorous! Until the lights came on, that is, until we shuffled out and the reality was there lined up, painted even more venomously in shit-colours for us to drag through, debilitated beyond words. Well, I speak for myself. As if to rub it in we passed a couple of morons at a street corner who kept lunging at each other and then one would let rip a rasping ugly laugh, and on our way in to the bus station a pack of kids on motorbikes came blarting up in full cry. I looked at Jan, who was plunging down the ramp on long strides, remote from me. I screwed up my face half-humorously at the din to convey comment— the skin of the world was corrupt, but that's nothing—and she just smiled faintly in a far-off, mysterious sort of fashion. Once again I was being tormented by a sense of failure, unable to make any contact or decide whose fault it was. This time at least it was obvious it wasn't just me to blame, but why couldn't I take the initiative, break through? It took passion to be heroic. I told myself glumly afterwards that I might have made the effort if she had interested me that much, which wasn't quite true as we sat side by side in the cinema, not touching, then on the bus locked in difficult, painfully stilted conversation, but by the time we'd walked through the village on stiff legs, past lighted windows, voices, a snatch of song from a radio, it was the truth. My personal universe was waiting, all I wanted was to plunge back into it.

The ache of remorse as I went to bed didn't last the night: once I'd let go of the nagging uneasy notion of us as a pair, things were much better. The whole menage seemed to relax and we either did things on our own or collectively that holiday, wandering on the rocks and pebbles of the beach looking for something special, glass, bits of driftwood, stones bored through by the sea, then on Sunday out for a jaunt to the Point—if you craned your neck you could see it from the cottage window—and we took it in turns pushing the pushchair up through the trees, the long peaceful track with its ruts and gulleys full of leaf mould, sea churning white in the steep rocky inlets below our feet. We'd get lungfuls of air and space, smell the leaf mould, Ray making mental notes to bring his saw as we sailed past thick branches lying dead and encrusted with lichen in the ferns. We went faster, tugged by that Point which always surprised us when we broke out of the trees and the gloaming on to the turf and outcrops—like being shot suddenly straight out to sea, or on the deck of a ship. Not a bay, not a cove, the open sea! Turning our backs on that and returning to the cottage, coming indoors to make a meal, involved a shrinking, it often seemed to me—we were so expanded and pleased with ourselves up there. Connie voiced it exactly, more than once, pouting and moving her limbs angrily, unbuckling the baby's strap and standing up with him seated on her forearm, bland as a Buddha.

'I don't wanna come in. Bloody cooking,' she'd say.

'Let's starve, then,' Ray said once, taking up the challenge. He was bent over folding up the pushchair flat like a sandwich, and I remember holding my breath for a second: I was hungry.

# 6

I'M WELL aware now that married women were my salvation. Girls were either too pure or too cagey, or a baffling mixture of both. How could you bring yourself to touch a girl who was so unsullied, who flushed and looked down at her feet or waited quivering like a sacrifice? And worse still were the brassy ones who had it all worked out in detail in advance, there it was ringing up in their cash-register eyes, your whole damn future: bungalow, carpet slippers, the little paddock in the rear where they let you canter to and fro with the lawnmower. Women were better. Women who'd been through the mill enough to be saddened, but they weren't defeated yet, only sharpened a little and wiser a lot: these were the ones with love and madness and generosity to spare if you could only find them.

I didn't find Aline, she was sitting quietly in the back of the junk shop. The printseller, that's how he described himself, introduced us. I knew him slightly, and it seemed they were old friends.

'Come and meet Aline,' he said, eyes gleaming. He liked to provide distractions for people.

There was no blinding flash or any of that nonsense, in fact we didn't go for each other at all at first. I made no real impression, she told me later. Honesty in a woman was something I hadn't encountered before: not this frontal kind.

'I wouldn't have looked twice at you in the street, to tell you the truth.'

I laughed: I knew I was safe.

For my part, I noted a pleasant, intelligent-looking woman with big eyes looking at me very steady and direct, with no particular curiosity or interest, nothing to spark me off.

'You had that vile blue serge suit on, you looked common, you could have been anybody,' she said.

'Clothes don't matter, do they?'

'They do to me, oh yes,' she said firmly.

'Alright, I'd got my disgusting suit on.'

'Then you and Lou invited me up to your flat for tea that Saturday and you came down the stairs to let me in—you were in that dark sailor's jersey thing, your brother's. You looked . . . different. What a difference! Soon as I set eyes on you that second time I thought—aha, what's this?'

I laughed again, felt absurdly privileged. It was a gift she had.

And it was letting her in from the street that I woke up to her, the luxuriance of her throat and shoulders, which the string of pearls seemed to confirm, the vibrant eagerness that wasn't flushing but a slight bending forward of the head, very young and touching—yet at the same time she was subtle, contained, rich and sad with her store of experience, smiling. It was a dank November afternoon, drizzly, but she was hatless, giving an umbrella a quick shake as she entered the hallway and presented me like a child with something in a paper bag: something heavy.

'My contribution,' she said happily.

'What's in it?' I said, surprised.

The stairs were narrow and she hadn't set foot in the house before so I led the way, the back of my body tinglingly aware of her.

'Nothing exciting—a tin of fruit,' she laughed.

'Ah yes, for the tea-party.'

'Is that all right?'

'What's that?'

'Is it enough? It's not much . . .'

'Yes, fine. Didn't expect anything. In a minute I'll just nip across the road for a loaf and some cakes.'

Gulping it out, but I had the excuse of the stairs.

And we'd got to our landing. I was aware for the first time of how poor it looked. Turned the corner to find Lou waiting in the doorway in silence, almost a resentful expression on his face. He'd heard us coming up.

'Here she is,' I said.

'Hallo,' she said brightly, if a little guarded.

'Cheers,' he said, ducking back inside.

He was there first, installed and waiting, so that gave him the upper hand. As if sensing this, Aline pushed out a remark to placate him.

'What do you do on Saturday afternoons as a rule?' she asked.

'Me?'

'Yes.'

'Have a snooze.'

'Oh dear!' she said.

He looked at her briefly. 'Why, what's up?'

'I'm disturbing your snooze.'

He shrugged and dropped down on the sofa, bang.

'Am I?' she asked, cool, her eyes animated.

'Don't be daft,' he said.

He could be like this, withdrawn, yet you could go on being relaxed and intimate with him as long as you knew the signs and didn't come too close. I'd seen him like this many a time. The touch of resentment could have been anything, perhaps he wanted to work, or wasn't in the mood to talk. I didn't care, it was exciting to have her in the room. It wasn't a room now, it was a stage: charged, electric. We made entrances, exits.

For a fortnight we'd lived in it, Lou and me, like a couple of monks. We had two rooms looking downhill to the station with its clock tower, and farther on the Council House, the trolleys went hissing past with a sound like acid spraying, the trees outside the big black church looked delicate and mysterious in winter, twigs lit up from underneath at night by the street lamps, half lost in fog in the mornings. Across the landing was the kitchen we shared with the Hungarian and his English wife, the couple who sublet the rooms to us. Lou was lolling on the lumpy old sofa with his legs spread out and a funny bent grin on his face: something was biting him. I began introducing him to Aline properly and she said, 'We know each other, Colin.'

Two surprises—the unexpected use of my name, which gave me a shock and I came very alert to her, and to find out that they were acquainted. Why hadn't Lou mentioned it, when I told him she was coming in for tea? I looked at him with fresh interest, puzzled, and he had the local paper spread on the floor in front of him and was hanging over it, reading—he liked doing that.

'I didn't realize that, Lou,' I said.

'Only to say how d'yer do—since going in the shop, like,' he mumbled, not raising his head or bothering to put any expression in his voice. He was a hard man to stare in the eye if he was set on being evasive, and this was one of those occasions: though his manner generally was flitting and quick, a will-o-the-wisp approach to life that kept him uninvolved and free and rolling, on the move always: like the buses he sprang into. He wouldn't walk anywhere if he could help it. In Nottingham you could walk down a street with him anywhere and see him nodding or waving to somebody—he seemed to know hundreds of people. So it was no surprise, when I considered it, him knowing Aline, and not to think it worth a mention was characteristic too. This apparent gregariousness which kept him (I nearly said saved him) from real contact with anybody, was it a philosophy he was working at, forming and nurturing it within himself, or a blind fear that was driving him? It wasn't a question you could ask him direct, he'd slip away under some jokey half-answer.

'How's the bread situation?' I asked him.

'Afraid the cupboard's bare, mate,' he said, still with his

head down and not a flicker of interest in his voice. You're overdoing it, I thought. Then he sat up: 'I could do with some fags if you're going over the shop. Hang about, I've got a quid here somewhere.'

'Have some of my cigarettes. Here!' Aline said, opening her handbag, and I flinched, she was being too nice to him in the mood he was in. He sounded curdled, best to let him be.

'Tips on 'em?' he said.

'Yes—have some, will you? Please.'

'Not tips,' he said shortly. 'Like smoking nowt.'

I was in sympathy with her big-heartedness, losing patience with the mingy spirit he was indulging.

'Shan't be a minute,' I said at the door and left them together, slipped down into the street that was quieter now with dusk settling into it, people going home to tea, a lull on the pavements, and I looked up at the living-room window, still unlit. I felt strangely elated at the thought of her up there, waiting.

Back up the stairs, rapid, and Lou was still at it, reading the bloody paper, but no sign of Aline. I tossed him his packet of ten and he said, 'Ta,' and I said, 'Where is she?'

'In the kitchen or having a slash, I dunno,' he said, still doing the hard act in a half-hearted way. I gave him up and went to look for her.

She was filling up the kettle at the sink, there was her fruit salad tin lifting its lid, she'd opened that and even got out plates, cups and saucers, cutlery. Home from home.

'That was quick,' she said. 'Shall I have the bread?'

'If you like,' and it was ridiculously easy to be with her, no strain, I couldn't believe it was happening to me. I avoided looking at her, this woman who was at my disposal.

'How do you like it, thick or thin?'

'Oh, average.'

She worked away, smiling faintly to herself: I saw that much.

'You don't come from around here, do you?'

'No,' I said.

'D'you like it, as a town?'

'It's not bad.'

'I grew up here. I've never been anywhere else,' she said simply.

I lit the gas under the kettle while she went on with things, and some silly chat passed between us about the shop on the corner, Gault's, where I'd been, and the treacle tart they sold there.

'You want to try it sometime, it melts in your mouth,' she said.

'I've got some,' I said, and we laughed. 'You must have been concentrating on it while I was over there.'

'No,' she said quickly, 'no I wasn't thinking of that.'

Something in her voice made me look at her, her eyes shone with her secret, and a kind of challenge, a tense defiance to her face that was beautiful and bare, shining like a knife blade. I couldn't face her, the kettle was on the boil so I saw to it, while she found the tray and loaded it up with our feast.

'Quite a spread,' I said, murmuring it. Whatever we said now was intimate, a sort of touching. My voice did it of its own accord. I couldn't help myself, I moved over to her by the kitchen table and picked up the tray, bowls glowing with glazed fruit in the thick white crockery. As if helplessly she reached out and touched my cheek, watching my face. I felt my eyes dark and soft on her, I was lissom, I had power and beauty for her in that moment, it went rippling over me. I astonished myself.

# 7

LOU COLTMAN was an elusive lad from the very beginning; pale haunted eyes that cast an immediate spell on me, said come on, live in a blaze of glory, it's all ours: he revelled in the power of his youth. His gift of intimacy came natural too, his whole face invited you, he couldn't help being personal, like the notes I had from him—then when you got there he'd gone, slipped away from you mysteriously. He'd always be a ghost. Small, lean, fair hair like a scrubbing brush on his forehead and later on a fringe of beard which made him somehow more boyish-looking than ever.

I'd been in Nottingham for months and I went one night to the Co-op hall, desperate for company, unable to bear the bed-sitting-room life I was leading, the creeping, creaking noises of other tenants, chained and padlocked doors, a woman sobbing one night, shouts, the hand-wringing despair I imagined: worst of all the four utterly blank walls of your own room as you opened the door at night and walked in, put down the milk bottle and it went *clonk*. The effort to accept that room sickened me, the terrible blankness of those walls drained the fight out of me. On the walls now were two watercolours I'd painted in there, God knows how: one a Pieta head, long big-nosed Mediterranean head in lime greens and bilious yellow and brown-pink, done blurry out of ignorance on too-wet paper and then liked for the effect. Thought I'd stumbled on a new technique. Now they looked dingy and in keeping with the general dirty-rags wretchedness of the house, unspeakably sad they looked at times like the chest of drawers, the blankets. I stared at them—the other was a bowl of fruit—and groaned, like a man who realises he's caught a dread disease. Melancholia. Leila said,

Do some painting, now you've got a room of your own. Or she may have said 'work'—I'd like to see some of your work. She spoke about art like a professional, had a great respect for it, whereas it seemed grotesque and choking to think of it in any other way except as something you did on the run between cataclysms, like making love. Thief art. But it was her prodding undoubtedly, my two-hours-a-week visitor from outer space—these meagre efforts were products of the old dispensation. Aline saw art as oceanic, a lush oriental sea growing, rising like wheat on the landscape, and her own melancholy would have told her that nothing grows in a bed-sitting-room.

And it was the same with writing, the impossibility of being a Writer today, complete with study and desk and wifey: surely nothing could be more absurd. Because there were connotations that went with that tranquil picture, you had to avoid like the plague those shameful inferences of authority, of speaking as a man of substance and weight, a little place in society and a little platform to clamber on, the spokesman, the man who judges, establishes directions, morals, gets listened to, taken account of. It didn't wash any more. Apply it to yourself, even with your eyes and ears shut tight to all the chaos, and you saw at once what a load of shit it was. Any writing had to be on the sly as it were, you weren't fit to judge, nobody was: the only thing you could possibly offer were mad songs, temptations, rules of survival for yourself—if anyone else found a use for them they were welcome, but it couldn't ever be created with a public in mind. No more, no more. You walked backwards and obliterated your footprints as you went, swearing blind it wasn't you, they must be mistaken. Artist? He went that way. Not me, never. Wouldn't be seen dead with him.

That was the message I had from Lou Coltman that night at the Co-op hall, and in some strange wafting fashion it came across without him saying a word, before the play-reading even started. I got very excited just looking at him. He was like a book you put off opening. You postpone it, you know what's in store for you. Sitting on the hard ordinary chair with his copy closed and such electric intensity about him, his hands and his head, I could hardly believe it. I wouldn't have cared if he hadn't opened his mouth all night, I sat gobbling him up. He sat there, composed, the essence of restraint, then it began and he was coiled like a spring, ready for freshness, savagery, abandon. What was it I found so riveting about him—they were reading this Strindberg thing, spiky and malicious, you tensed yourself for cruelty and got pierced with tenderness—what was the galvanic quality he had surging off him, a mixture of nervy, abject panic and the most devastating contempt and rage and held-back passion? He was the producer, too: I might have guessed. About forty of us in the audience, no more, and I kept glancing to left and right through the performance but not a flicker of the electricity I was receiving seemed to register on the others. Sat there like lumps of wood, clapped dutifully at the end as if measuring it out on their palms, and I wanted to grab their collars and shake a storm of rapture out of them, I wanted to signal a message back, acknowledge that here was somebody aware of an extraordinary event.

What I actually did, I slunk out with the rest of them into the pouring rain, tramped back to my room, splashing along pavements hunched up with my raincoat collar turned up and buttoned, conjuring up in my head his appearance, movements rather than the tone of his voice, trying to fathom the nature of this amazing throw-away power of his. I ended up scribbling him a fan letter: really a letter of thanks for existing, making it happen, whatever it was—it came out pretty incoherent so I left it like that. Why not? What was there to say after all except thanks and how fantastic to stumble on an oasis in a city I'd thought was dry as a rock?

Next thing was, the pallid pop-eyed lady on the ground floor, half out of her mind with her seven kids and her husband in the navy, she was yelling up the stairs in the frantic hysterical screech she used for her family to tell me to come down, I had a visitor. Saturday afternoon; it was a wonder I was in. Thought it must be a mistake because I didn't know anybody: apart from Leila, nobody knew I was here, I might as well have been dead. I was like a ghost walking, no name, no identity, if the front door had been locked I could have floated through the walls. Who the hell could it be?

Lou Coltman stood on the pavement, hanging back, half defiant and half indifferent, or sheepish—I was never sure. Smaller, slighter than I'd remembered, slouchingly cocky about the head and shoulders, fag in his mouth.

'Got your note,' he said, and twitched slightly round the eyes: very slightly but I saw it.

'Yes—I'd forgot—can you come up?' I gabbled.

'After you, mate,' he said, coming forward. Just a touch of mockery, but no sneering. Friendly, curious, and when he moved, eager. Hair creamed and not having it, bristling up at the front, shoes sharp and scuffed, trouser ends a bit tatty-looking. Crisp white shirt and dark tie like a piece of rag, knotted anyhow.

Upstairs he seemed utterly indifferent to my ugly room. Sat on the edge of my bed, on the grey army blanket, leaned forward with his legs apart and concentrated on his cigarette: or on whatever he was thinking. Staring down at the floor. I waited, swam around in the silence, bathed in optimism, saying things to myself like this: Look who's here! Look what the wind's blown in! He was sitting and smoking. It was funny—I began to wonder what he'd come for: maybe just a sit down. But it was merely to establish contact. He did that all the time, made contact and then waited. His philosophy, if you could call it that, was summed up in one rule: Never push anything. After a while I found his waiting game unnerving and said, 'How about a cup of tea?'

'Coffee me, if you've got some,' he said flatly.

'Yes, plenty--I'll put the kettle on then.'

'No milk,' he said.

The cooker was outside the door on the landing, a communal one, my Woolworth's tin kettle on the flaky iron grid, up to now my one cooking utensil. Might get a saucepan one day to boil an egg in, but I recoiled from any suggestion of permanency, anything that might look as though I were setting myself up in this house. I was finding out how superstitious I was, afraid to tempt fate. Hop, skip and jump down to the turn in the stairs, where a yellow triangle of sink was snug in the corner, under a narrow window—that's where I had to go to fetch water. Twist the tap and it sputtered and slushed like an old man talking through ill-fitting dentures, then it filled your kettle in a series of steady retches. Or if somebody had a tap on somewhere in the depths of the house, all you got was a faint strangling sound and you had to wait. Water this time, retch, retch, and it almost had a merry splash to it now, with a visitor waiting upstairs. My first. Life could be something, even here. I didn't need to look, I could tell by the weight when I had enough water in.

I offered him some bread and cheese, tomato, lettuce leaf, but he wasn't interested.

'This is smashing.'

Thighs parted, he sucked gingerly at the hot coffee, glanced sideways at the newspaper he'd laid out on the blanket beside him, poking vague disinterested questions at me, long intervals in between.

'So you wrote me a note,' he said, 'just like that.'

'That's it.'

Now and again he flicked glances at me surreptitiously. Sly or shy, I couldn't decide.

'Often do things like that, do you? Straight off, I mean?'

'No, not exactly,' I laughed. 'Never done it before.'

Which made him look properly, with real interest and respect.

'Good, I like that,' he said with relish, and I sparkled, felt good, responding at once.

'You do?' came out of me, and I despised it for what it was, worldly, cagey, nothing to do with how I felt.

'Yeh, that's how I like things to happen, off the cuff like that. Random.'

'I know what you mean,' I said coolly, waiting.

He stuck his pale young face forward, pugnacious, alive to the implications of this idea, suddenly very positive and breezy, evangelistic even.

'If you'd gone away and thought about it for a week, mulled it over, considered it from every angle and *then* done something about it—supposing you had—it wouldn't have been the same at all,' he said.

I considered this speech: it was quite a mouthful for him.

'Wouldn't it?' I said (or some devil in me), merely to egg him on.

He shook his head very seriously, swelled out his bottom lip, juicy red, grotesque.

'Not the same.'

Abstracted, his eyes wandered down to his newsprint again.

To jolt him I said stubbornly, 'Not if I used exactly the same words?'

Again his head shook in the stubborn veto: 'If you get a sudden impulse and say to your girl friend, luv ya, that's not like going off for a fortnight, weighing up the pros and cons and then posting it in a bloody letter, is it?'

I grinned. 'You said a week.'

A second ago it was as if the living universe hung waiting for answers, now he slumped over on one elbow, rummaging for fags in his right-hand pocket, affecting a bored air. 'Don't let's flog it.'

'No,' I said.

I felt the lonely shiver in the chest that comes with withdrawing, with presuming too much, too soon.

'Good cuppa.'

'Fancy some more?'

'Not me. You have what you want.'

But I just waited emptily, not unhappy, while he smoked and furrowed his forehead, tussled inside himself and finally came up with—'Each day ought to be a blank sheet of paper in front of you, waiting for scribbles, nothing mapped out beforehand. That's how it ought to be.'

'It is for me, more or less.'

With a queer touch of contempt or pique, as if I'd tried to steal his thunder, he said, 'You're home and dry then, no problems.'

'Think so?'

He nodded vigorously, inhaling.

'It's the forcers every time, they're the ones who bugger things up.'

Afterwards he said restlessly, 'Coming in town?' and this again was typical. He had to have movement, people, talk: city life was a river and he was an out-and-out city man, a nomad, he liked to feel it swirling round him and be in touch, yet left free. He was sure of himself. His element was rootlessness, he was born to it. For me this was a completely new attitude, it meant that the amenities of a city were there to be used, exploited, they were on tap like the water and electricity, waiting and ready, you switched on, plunged in. Dipped in and out. Got on a bus and swirled into the centre, lying back on the side seat as Lou did now, looking as if he owned the place. The bus was his. He lolled back, impudent, a kid of twenty-odd. The interesting thing was that this attitude didn't make him international, but intensely local. A local patriot. He took a pride in the streets, pubs, buses, these things he used like an owner. In the next county they were different. He wasn't there, he was here. The environment he was using became his, made over. Not the planners, the builders, but the users created the cities. Knowing this gave him his local pride.

I'd always felt hostile or bleak or unspeakably dreary in cities: now I saw they had a certain glamour. I looked at Lou and grinned. Never push anything. He twitched his lips faintly and let his eyes rest on me for a second, then he was gazing out of the window again.

# 8

WE GOT off in the square and went drifting across the open space from one side to the other as if we weren't going anywhere. I kept with him, we exchanged one or two basic questions—'Been here long?'—'Where you from?'—and it turned out he'd been a student teacher in Coventry and chucked it after the first taste of teaching practice. Now it was summer, the evening had that suspended feeling warm air brings, the sky pearly-feathery and absolutely still over the Council House, but Lou hadn't seen it. He was hunched, down-looking. Nothing higher than a poster interested him: certainly not nature. For landscapes to mean anything to him they had to be man-made. I asked him why he jacked in the teaching and he shrugged, off-hand, without answering.

'The pub up here near the castle's alright. Depends which night though. What day is it?'

'Saturday, thank God.' A remark that was more habit than truth. Since coming here and living in a bedsitter I'd come to dread the yawning hole of the weekend.

'Saturday's alright as a rule.'

Then as we went mooching uphill in a queer silence he suddenly started on my question, saying as if to himself that education was a waste of time, he had a built-in resistance to it, like religion: the instant he got inside the school on his preliminary visit and saw them herding around as if it meant something deadly serious, it frightened him. He'd escaped from this world, he'd forgotten what a straitjacket it was. Without knowing why, he'd been running ever since, become a freedom addict. Seeing them in Assembly being screwed into rigid rows and hushed and then told to sing loud, sing properly or else by some thin-lipped, pasty-faced grizzled fogey, it was too much, it took him back in a sickening rush to his own schooldays which he'd loathed and dreaded and then immediately forgotten.

'What did me good and proper though was the Staff Room.'

'How's that?'

'That's where you saw it was a job of work and nowt else. I mean these teachers were trapped in a situation and trying to make the best of it, to get through to pay-day, pension-day—they cuffed kids round the earhole if they were that sort, they gave 'em debates now and then if they were that sort, but you only had to see them there stirring their mugs of tea for it to hit you that they weren't no different from you or me—or the bloody kids. All the guff about marks, progress, improvement, Johnny's got it in him if we can only winkle it out, you saved that for Parents' Day and Speech Day and when you put in for your next rung up—nobody believed in it for itself. It really got me, and it was so plain, and no need for a soul to mention it. You just looked.'

We pushed into the pub, which was dingy and brown, iron stanchions at the corners of the bar, those chairs with round plywood seats and holes punched in a pattern—the kind they used to have in offices—and an old upright piano, lid down and locked, in the corner black as a coffin. There was a fireplace, grate full of ashes, an old woman sitting up close to the hearth as if she could feel the warmth of last winter's fires, sucking down a Guinness slowly and twisting the scrag of her body to look at whoever was coming in, with a kind of blind beakishness. The public bar this was and it looked deserted, just the man behind the counter wiping a glass and giving us a nod, thin and yellow like a candle with a meagre black wick of hair, shirt sleeve dragging in the wet. This was the old-fashioned brown pub, the local, it had regulars and was tucked away in a back street, in a district marked down for slum clearance in the foggy future. We went around a glazed screen and down an alley of a passage, stone-flagged, into a poky room with wood settles.

'Take a pew,' Lou muttered, moving over to a corner, 'and meet this bloke, Woody . . . I'll be back. He's a good lad, Woody.'

And I'd lost him, he went and attached himself to one group in the middle of the room, said a few words, stood listening at their elbows and merging, hanging his head, completely unassertive and colourless, then went drifting off into an elbow of the room where I couldn't watch him. Not that Woody gave me the chance: he was the buttonholing sort. I began to wonder if I'd bumped into him before, but of course I hadn't. Apparently the mere fact that we both knew Lou Coltman was enough for him. I took a dislike to him on sight, that narrow face and flushing skin over the cheekbones, china-blue eyes and a corrupt loose little baby mouth curling up at one side as he poured out talk and appreciated himself—'I tell a fucking good story, don't I, bloody amusing, don't you think I'm clever the way I embroider it, on form tonight I am'—this was what his wide eyes with no bottoms to them seemed to be saying. I sat listening to him or pretending to, let him rattle on, searching for Lou out of the corner of one eye and trying to work out what he saw in this mate of his. Woody lowered his voice, confiding.

'If you want a woman,' he was advising me, 'I can put you on to a beauty. She might be in later: I'll introduce you if you like—but you want to watch out, there's some real old rampers come in here, really thick they are. I mean, you don't want to die of boredom getting to it do you? I know I don't. If you fancy coming to a pub called *The Odd Wheel* down Alfreton Road I'll show you a bitch in there I went with once—just for a laugh, you know? I'm a writer, did Lou tell you? I work on the *Post* but I don't mean the sort of crap I do in there for a living—I'm writing a book as a matter of fact. You'll get the impression I'm a big-headed bastard, but listen, Colin—can I call you Colin?—I only mention it because I like to observe people, if you know what I mean. Anyway there's this gin-drinking fanny at *The Odd Wheel* who always comes sidling round me, jigging her big tits in her jumper—no brassiere, you can see the nipples stuck out—rubbing her thighs up against me on the seat, you wouldn't believe it if you didn't see it for yourself. Forty if she's a day and one of those bloody stupid pony tails in an elastic band, and when she opens her gob, oh my Gawd. "Hallo, duck, interesting place this, isn't it. Haven't seen you here before"—incredible make-up, pure fantasy, and out of it comes this mashed-up accent, and I think, "Who do you think you're kidding, you're on the machines at Players you are, Clara" . . . That's her name, Clara, believe it or not. So one night I'm half sloshed—I mean you'd have to be—and we go up to her place, a flat she calls it. What a slut, you'd think there'd been a murder in there, it was pure chaos. Kids yelling in prams in one corner, plaster seagulls going up the wall, sink jammed solid with dirty crocks and in the midst of all that she disappears and comes trapesing out half stripped, nellies hanging out of some gory red lace thing—and she starts clearing the debris off the settee. I made some excuse, I just couldn't stomach it, not even pissed . . .'

'Sounds nasty,' I said, grinning him off, and for something to say: but he was eyeing a couple of girls, newcomers, working up a little spiel on them. It was going to be the same lip-licking, eye-gleaming performance, and the thought came: there's something not quite right about you. As if he hated women almost, was intent on having some sort of revenge. I spied Lou weaving through with the beers and packets of peanuts, flushed with all his encounters.

I sat on the bench as Lou came up and Woody pushed himself up closer to say, dropping his voice intimately, his eyes leery, 'Lou said you'd written him a great letter.'

I mumbled something, fobbed him off with false modesty,

but he humiliated me obscurely and I didn't understand why. There's something nasty about you, I thought, and left it at that. I understand better now. Without knowing a thing about me he was itching to pay me compliments, flatter me, for some weird reason of his own. Praise of any kind makes me uneasy—who can sit inside me and measure the worth of what I do or am?—and senseless praise that sucks up can take away your pride and self-respect if you aren't careful. Praise me and I duck, back away, make off for cover. To be recognised is my constant need. Praise implies blame, the same critical coin: somebody is coming up warily with a certain detachment, carrying calipers and a little book for your measurements, notes on your performance. For the future. Never for what you are. To be recognised is to be loved for what you are, for your weaknesses. Recognise me and I sparkle, begin to recover, want to excel, to expand.

'Now then,' said Lou, introducing, 'you know Woody, that's him you've been speaking to, and this is Bob, him with the big glass and nothin' in it—and next to him there looking angelic, only she ain't, is Maureen.'

'Shurrup you,' Maureen said, blonde and gormless-eyed, heavy low fringe touching her eyebrows. She had a bewildered expression. She giggled. She seemed to like Lou, but wasn't anything to do with him. She was with Bob, a big brawny fellow with a hot baked face and scrubby Van Gogh beard, in a thick green sweater and no shirt. He had his arm draped round her shoulders, they made a placid peaceful couple on that side of the table.

'Who wants a nail in 'is coffin?' Bob said genially, offering his packet of Capstans.

'Don't smoke, thanks,' I said, thinking for the first time that it would be hard not to in a gathering like this, if you intended to stay friendly. The sociability of this man came off him like a heat. I felt a pang of shame at my meanness in denying him pleasure. Cigarettes were passed out, the others lit up, and then I was aware of being fixed. It was Bob watching me with all his head like a dog, eyeballs bulged in concentration.

'Let me guess,' he said, smiled, rubbed the side of his face and it rasped.

'What's that?' I said warily, a bit foxed by the way he'd said it, importantly.

'You ent local?'

'No.'

'Brummy?'

I nodded. 'Near enough.'

'See?' He turned in triumph to the girl. 'Good, en I.'

'Tek it easy,' she said. 'Steady on, kid.' To me she said confidentially, 'Don't worry, duck, he don't mean no harm.'

'Harmless, is he?' I laughed.

'Wanna try me?' Bob said to the girl.

She blew smoke in his face. 'Hark at it,' she said.

Bob wasn't finished with me yet.

'You're an actor,' he said.

I shook my head. Maureen let out a shriek. 'Yah, clever dick!'

Bob shook his head slowly, sank back away from me, vaguely friendly but puzzled. I was glad the pressure was off.

'I could 'a swore you was an actor,' he said.

Then he lost interest in me.

'Anybody who wants to buy me a pint, don't worry about hurtin' me feelings,' he announced, cheerful and clomping. 'I'm broke I am. Broke an' happy.'

'On a Saturday?' said Lou, already on his feet and reaching for the glass.

'Had me pay packet pinched, all but a quid,' Bob said, without a flicker of complaint.

'Why didn't you say so?' Lou said, going, and when he got back he said, 'That'll teach you not to trust your fellow workers.'

The man was on building, a labourer, but apparently he'd been a skilled fitter at Raleigh's and couldn't stand the indoor life. I was sitting with eyes and ears wide open, all my senses, as you tend to do when nothing's happening, you seem to be drifting pointlessly, yet sense the possibility of creative moments. Lou was the unknown quantity, that was his fascination—he was attending and yet looking out for somebody, another person, a further ingredient. 'That'll teach you . . .' he said softly and then ducked over his pint to listen and wait, as if he'd dropped in a catalyst. I saw what he was: a ginger man.

'How d'you mean?' said Bob, genuinely shocked. 'I got some good mates on the job – one sneaky bastard don't change everything. What d'you mean, that'll teach me?'

'Well, it will, won't it,' squeaked Maureen, and I looked at her and then saw Lou with such a secret little smile at his mouth corners, his head down. He'd started something, it was fizzing. Trivial, but he had to have a stir around him. And he was passing time, expecting others.

'Teach you not to leave cash in your jacket,' put in Woody sarcastically, but he wasn't really interested.

'Agreed,' said Bob heavily. 'But that's not what Lou said.'

'I take it back,' Lou murmured, then became suddenly emphatic, intense: a startling transformation. 'Would you trust this bloke?' he asked, and gave a nod at me.

Bob put back his head and laughed. 'How the hell would I know, I never met him before!'

'I mean by looking at him,' Lou said.

I sat squirming while they all focused on me. If I hadn't been on the receiving end, if it had been someone else, it would have been comical. I might even have enjoyed it.

'Yes,' Bob said at last, 'I would, mate.'

'How's that, then?' Lou persisted.

Bob looked puzzled, he frowned like a boy.

'What makes you so sure?' Lou said.

Now it was the other's turn. The limelight scorched him. Watching this Bob and grinning at him encouragingly, I suddenly noticed his wide belt round his trousers, it was made of red webbing, a big brass buckle at the front: a fancy belt. I looked at him with fresh interest and thought, he's not just a clod, this one. He fancies himself. Somehow this new aspect of him caught me by surprise because he sat all in a heap, unshapely, no self-consciousness and no vanity. But I'm wrong, I thought.

'How?' he said, mouthing. 'It's easy. It's bleedin' obvious, I'd say.'

'Yeah, but why?' Lou urged, not asking so much as extracting, like a hypnotist with his trance victim. It was amazing how he could soothe and stroke with his voice and at the same time convey force, insistence, the pressure of his will. I kept my ears cocked, marvelling. Bob was too thick to respond, I felt: it was me, watching, I was the one who sat spellbound.

Bob itched about and worked his shoulders uneasily, he would have spat in his hands if that could have helped. He stumbled blindly into speech, saying in a harsh voice that the police only bashed you up if you were a certain type, they knew who to pick and who to leave alone, and it was the same with him, he could smell the bastards who would shop you, shit on you . . . He sat back with his glass in his fist, white curds clinging to his lips, his speech floundering. 'It's obvious, Lou, obvious,' he said, almost fuming.

Now, as Woody opened his mouth, Lou looked over his shoulder again for whoever he was expecting: maybe hoping to see somebody he could borrow from. In seconds we'd be in the middle of a hot debate on the police, whether you needed courage to be a copper, the brutality, the squalor of the profession, was it forced on them or did they lap it up, and what rights did you have, if any, when they grabbed you and you were broke and no fixed abode—what chance did you have?

I had little to contribute, apart from a bobby jumping out of a hedge when I was a kid, riding a bike down a country lane and not stopping at the halt sign. I was with a great friend, a boy several yards behind me, who had time to brake. With him as witness, my pride flamed up and I found enough courage to act stubborn when the copper tried to make me look foolish. 'Now then,' he said, planted like a tree before my front wheel, 'you could see the sign, you're not blind, so why didn't you stop?'

'I didn't see it,' I said, which was the truth.

The policeman let his gaze rest on me for a long time but I didn't wilt, not with my friend watching. 'How old are you?' he said, heavily sarcastic. I went hot in the face and said, 'I don't see what that's got to do with it,' and in a flash he dropped his baiting game, yanked out his notebook and took my name and address. My old man paid the fine. I mentioned this when Lou brought up about power and how it could corrupt. But *he* had a power, I felt it. He kept looking towards the door but his other mates didn't come. After a while he muttered something about making a phone call and disappeared. He was gone for an hour. The others thought he was round the corner in *The Iron Man*, another pub he was known in. When he came back he was edgy, strangely subdued: at closing time he was ready to shove off with hardly a word. I asked for the address where he was living.

'Hang about,' he said, ransacked his jacket, which looked slept in, and came out with a crumpled buff envelope. I gave him my pen and he scrawled on the paper, using his palm as a rest, holding the pen lightly and a long way from the tip. I wasn't surprised by this fastidiousness, nor by the nervy style of his handwriting. 'Cheers then, mate,' he said, already loping for a bus he'd spotted. The bus stop was right down the street but he made it. He didn't look back.

## 9

A MUCH more uncomplicated man is Davey, who comes later but can't wait . . . 'a fanatic', his girl calls him. She doesn't mean that exactly, she's referring to his mad impulses, and when I say uncomplicated, compared with Lou, I don't mean he's simple. I often wish I could have seen them together, but never did: just have to accept that they knew each other.

Like Lou, Davey has the gift of immediate intimacy, you trust him, but unlike Lou he overwhelms you with warmth, fraternity, opens up like a child, gives himself away completely. Lou's personal alright, but even when he appears to be revealing, stripping, he conceals. Every step he takes has the effect of covering up his tracks. So with Lou I'm none the wiser about him, I still don't know what makes him tick. Davey is utterly transparent, all his actions betray him: it's impossible not to know. And right from the beginning I was aware of him physically, still glowing all over with the nimbus of adolescence, though he was twenty-three or four, his voice very expressive, huskily emotional, his whole attitude to life ridiculously fragile and tender, so you caught your breath and thought, what's this: I must be dreaming. As if to counteract this—though you couldn't say he was aware of it as a grave weakness, he was one big weakness—he'd anchor himself, prevent himself from floating away in sheer joyousness, or sad smoke-rings, grievings after childhood idylls, by slinging dollops of verbal shit right and left. And by a nimble goon humour of his own, and being a clever mimic, he could mix his qualities on his tongue and achieve a union, though it sounds crazy, impossible. He was an earthy romantic, an idealist who farted, who had to keep drawing your attention to the sheer shittiness as well as the creatureliness of existence. If it hadn't been for the laugh that went with it you'd have sworn it was a kind of disgust he had for reality, a rage. His dreams flowered, the heroes of his youth were glorified in the news cuttings he showed me, then the world he saw through the window shattered it, outraged him. Except that he laughed a lot, sparkled visibly, groaned with pleasure when he was hungry and his girl Judy shoved a plate of beans and chips in front of him, some doorstop brown bread and a mug of hot tea, syrup-sweet. He'd scoop up a mouthful on his fork, load his bread, take a huge bite, groan, mumble 'Ah lovely little un' and put his arm round her waist, then curse when she sat down with a bump on his lap before he'd finished, maybe banging noses as she coiled like a cat and tried to kiss his greasy mouth. 'Not on me chops, not when I'm eatin'.' He'd jab her away brutally and say 'Gerroff, you stupid bitch, now look what you've done!'

I'd wait for the bang, knowing her temper, just sitting there as if invisible, but it was amazing, nothing happened except a slight feeling of strain in the atmosphere, and Judy would be back at the cooker or the sink and Davey would clumsily, sheepishly begin to mend the relationship. 'Sorry, little un,' he'd say, still eating, 'you know I ent got much time, I got to get back to the fuckin' grindstone—you know that, don't you, duck?' And she'd come back, coil on his lap and perch there, still as a dove, and I'd blink and grin my head off, I couldn't help it; but nobody would notice me, they'd be cooing and kissing and he'd say, 'You're so bloody clumsy that's your trouble—oh Christ me nose still hurts' and she'd croon, 'Oh Davey, I'm sorry, does it,' and soothe his hair. Then the kettle would boil over and he'd yell, 'Now look!' Suddenly he'd take care of me with a warm glance, a tender grin, a solicitous remark—'How's Colin in the corner—fancy another cup of tea, me old wack?'

Lou was elusive physically as he was in other respects. I

once saw him stripped at the sink in the kitchen of his mother's house, having a wash down, and there was nothing deep-chested or athletic about him but he was surprisingly muscular round the shoulders, and dangling from his neck he had a St Christopher on a chain. His vigour in some curious way didn't make you conscious of his body. Whereas Davey was a body in blossom, he flowered from the waist, his life branched down through his long legs to the girls he needed, they sapped him or renewed him, he was never sure whether it was death or rebirth. He thrashed his arms, held his head, complained bitterly of their possessiveness. A tender, bighearted animal—then you noticed his hands, his fingers, delicate and shapely and narrow, feminine hands, and it was this that reminded you of his agile mind. I met him first in the summer and he wore nothing much, cotton drill pants and a sweatshirt, baseball shoes. I could smell the salt on his skin, he'd roared off to Skeggy on his motorbike. His blond hair was in spikes. 'Ain't it funny,' he said, 'they let you swim in the sea and yet that water's international. Touches all them countries. You'd think they'd want to stamp your bleedin' passport before you put your big toe in even.'

He drove a bread van round the country districts outside Derby, but he'd been a factory apprentice like me and jacked it in, then he was a signal-box boy on the railway and loved it, gazing out of the window high up on spring mornings, hearing a blackbird every evening pouring out liquid ecstasy. That was when he started his dreams, buried in that cutting, lovely, with a signalman who reminded him of his grandfather. They transferred him to another box, the man there was a mean pot-bellied bastard, too miserable to live, Davey was on early shift and kept turning up late, so miseryguts soon had his knife into him . . .

I'm missing something out that's vital, I still haven't got the picture. Those hands. The strangeness and beauty of his voice sometimes, when he was rapt, quivering to communicate a memory that had grown precious, a key to his world: yet he just missed being a street-corner yobbo. His heart would swell and choke him just before his hips began to swagger. He had a funny collection of pals: delinquents, thickies, students, misfits like me—his warmth didn't discriminate. Slowly it dawned on you how gregarious he was, how you were part of the swarm, the changing pattern, and this hurt, because you could have sworn the intimacy had been personal, secret, just for you. That was laughable, you saw that in the end. He made contact all over his body, all the time, gave off a kind of helpless love: did it as easily as he moved through the air. Before he knew what had happened he'd be clustered with mates, stuck with them, all kinds, like burrs on the legs of your trousers, and another side of him would surge up in reaction—the solitary. 'All I want is to be by myself, think my own bloody thoughts,' he'd say, confiding in me because I didn't seem a threat like the others, I left him free. But I was the biggest threat: I loved him.

I saw him as physical all the time, his hair growing down to his neck, his jaunty-bashful walk, shirt open and no vest, the run of blond hair coming up from his belly-button, but never myself bared to him physically as a homosexual does. The girls took him naked and emptied him, he poured out his love for them from between his legs, complete and utter, and I was the same, my balls and cock ached after the moist secret entrances of women. Once he said to me on a brief camping trip, we stood shoulder to shoulder unpacking stuff and his voice came small and colourless, his face rueful: 'Ah Colin, there's no way to express your love for a man.' He wanted to put his arm round me, it was spontaneous and beautiful and I couldn't help him, I was paralysed by the unwritten rules. Afraid too of looking a clown. It should have been natural, it could have been. It was fraternal.

Judy was his regular, he more or less lived with her, but girls and women fell for him all over the place and he just responded: nothing nasty or grabbing in him, he loved their girlness, femaleness, their pliant bodies, willing natures, the sympathy that shone in their eyes, their tears, and oh their smiles, how he loved the way they smiled at him. He would have gone through the world of men cutting the same kind of swathe, I'm certain, except for the hard edge of male assertion he came up against, and of course his own male will clashing, conflicting, bringing a vindictive, bitter streak out in him that I hated to see. He approached everyone, male and female, young and old, as if there was no difference, he melted them if he could with his warmth, he went forward barebreasted, all heart. Mere humanity in a person was enough to inspire generosity in him, and the more lavish their weaknesses, the better he liked it. He responded to anything generous, he expanded visibly. Naturally he was bound to get in a mess and it couldn't last, the world being what it is: he spoiled rapidly as the adjustment twisted him, he fell into ugly jeering moods and you felt it was indecent to be with him, a silent witness. Then he'd recover and come bursting into a room and it was like old times, he'd be radiant, open-faced, he'd sweep you off your feet.

## 10

IF I had to put into one word my loathing for the society I grew up in, I'd say, without hesitation: sex. To find sex torn out of context and isolated in medical books, picked over by psychologists, worst of all hung like bloody meat in shop windows, stamped for sale and paraded on the slave blocks, made over into a pornography of precision and detachment by cameras—here was the root of my hatred for adults. I saw that thrillers, gutter press, advertising, they were all at the same game of striptease, the whole masturbatory culture we have now at full blast was just getting under way. But the disembowelling was still to come. The snouts in the money-troughs hadn't yet understood that a new source of wealth could be made to flow, that all it needed for the fires to burn, for the revolution to take place, for the smelting of sex to begin, were a few hundred furnaces of sick lust roaring away up and down the land. To grow up to manhood in the midst of that burning lava is to be in hell, is crucifixion. It's the beginning of the end when sex is separate, when it carries a price tag. We're going to hell when you can pick sex up in your hand and fit a french letter on it. We're sex-mad because we think sex is detachable, like a dog running round in a frenzy trying to gobble its own tail. What we call sexy is something we can lick up off the surface of our skins with our tongues, an oily sauce which is no more than the sweat bursting from us as we run between the furnaces.

When one desire in your blood runs hot for the throbbing image of bloody meat hung on hooks in the shop window, the sex thing smelted out by the furnaces, and another desire burns for the love of a particular woman, for her voice, her tender solicitude, her proud haunchy walk, the hollow of her back, the thoughts in her head, the laughter in her throat, the spittle in her mouth, the shit in her colon, then you are torn apart in the very centre of your being, you are crucified.

I was twenty-three when I went with the prostitute. London was the right place, ripe and rotten with prostitution: everybody was at it in one way or another. You could smell the sex-and-money mixture, it had its own sound, tinkly and clanging, the stink of petrol and steel and burnt rubber in the streets went with the Cockney rat-yap on the corners, the cold shoulder in the tube stations, the boot in the alley. Everything on sale and going cheap, even death zipping in and out on wheels, blaring like a car roof in the sun.

I was in a crowded tube with a suitcase, it was the rush hour and passengers stood up like skittles all round the doors. We slid in to Earl's Court and a weasel of a man lashed out viciously with his foot at my case, snarled 'Get it out of the way' and came bundling through, using his shoulders, making for the door. I was too flabbergasted and at that time too timid to answer, I just felt sick all through my blood, wished him dead and loathed the whole carriageful of wall-eyed zombies, myself included. Then the curving posters on the tunnels with their chorus of con-messages, then the multitudes on the escalators, the maniacs who have to run, the ticket collectors who look malignant, the sophisticated, bored, languid and predatory faces, the cigar in the juicy red mouth, the glossy briefcase, the jewelled finger dripping blood, the blazing arrogance of the poor: and you get out through the nearest bolt-hole and it's no different, but at least there's the sky with its space.

For a young man longing for something wonderful to happen to him there's a terrible atmosphere inside even a feeble place like the Windmill, for instance. Coming out he feels soiled right through, tainted for ever. What's worse, the wonderful something he strains towards with his longing seems a kingdom he can't possibly enter now that his purity is lost. He's corrupt. All he's done is sat in this crappy old theatre where the nudes aren't allowed to move, and no opera glasses, no cameras, illustrated programmes are five bob at the entrance, the show's continuous (we never closed) and at every interval the old rams at the back go leaping over the seats in a mad dash for the empty front row. For the young man the show is one long humiliation. He's from the provinces, nobody knows him in here: even so he feels conspicuous. He sneaks glances to right and left. Men only, in all directions. The comedians hurl themselves on and they grimace with pain, struggle desperately, laugh bleakly at their own jokes, up against a blank wall of brutal indifference. The rows of Shylocks wait like butchers for the flesh. Their eyes sharpen. On it comes, prancing and oh so English, titties fresh from boarding school bounce gaily in the transparent blouses. You can see the cherry doing a jig, mostly civilised, one or two really loose and frantic, but even so in the best possible taste. You don't know which to concentrate on. The singing which falls out of their chops as they pant up and down in a line is excruciating, the accents so genteel that you have to make a conscious effort to ignore it: like the piano twinkling in palm court style through the set-pieces, where they have a nude standing motionless at the back being bathed in coloured light and you try to tell yourself it's a woman, she's bollock-naked and that's her belly-button but it's no good, she looks no more real and warm than a bronze lump on the Embankment.

You're only young once, they tell you, but being young can be agony. Funny as well, when you look back. A pal told me he had a girl friend in Leicester who was churchy, and when they were lying in the grass one summer she asked him, 'Do you believe in intercourse before marriage?' 'No,' he said, and he had a stalk on him halfway up to his neck. 'No, neither do I,' she said, and took him home to tea. Somehow he got his erection jammed in under his belt or somewhere, and he sat there squirming in the sitting room with her mother's beady eye fixed on the stain between his legs. 'Oh bloody hell it was funny,' he said, telling it, and I'd like to bet it wasn't.

I didn't know where the prostitutes hung out, I hadn't asked any of my mates at the factory: that would be giving the game away, and the truth was, I hadn't admitted even to myself that I was going to try and get picked up by one. Even in London all day, mooching past the galleries and bookshops, squatting on stools in the snack bars and watching through the mirrors, the swarm and blur of the crowd, I still didn't know. When it got dark I began to know. Went drifting down those side streets behind Piccadilly like one of the damned, then it drizzled and the black road between the pavements glazed and ran. I stood in a doorway watching the odd car swish through, heart thumping up violently whenever a woman went past. I was doing it, I knew now. Waiting. I wanted the vultures to swoop and pick me off, I was that tense and desperate. A car swung in to the gutter opposite and stopped, engine throbbing, a figure moved out of the doorway, the car door opened and closed, they roared away. A pick-up. So this was it, it was here, I was on the circuit. Still nothing happened. A young couple went by, lovers, coiled together and heads bare, heedless in the rain. I watched dumbly. Their innocence pierced me, the cruel simplicity of their lives, they splashed round the corner and I stared into the utter bleak emptiness of the street. In the factory an apprentice would say of his sweetheart, 'She's fabulous.' He'd have to tell you. Then he had to coarsen it, and the acrid touch, the humour and contempt. 'She's fabulous,' he'd say—'I could use her shit for toothpaste.'

When she came up I wasn't ready: I didn't see where she sprang from. There she was sauntering by, perfectly natural, saying 'Chilly, darling?' or some such stock phrase.

Holding an umbrella. She sounded foreign. I nodded, perhaps mumbled a word, and it was fateful, overwhelmingly important as I stepped towards her and she held the umbrella over me.

'What a miserable evening!' she said brightly, as we walked on side by side like husband and wife, the umbrella floating above our union, while I shivered in my chest and moved my legs in a tension. It was happening, happening. You moved your legs and it happened.

'Here we are!' she said, stopping at a green door, and from her handbag she took a key. 'That wasn't far, was it?'

Now I was her child: she was mothering me. I followed her in through the doorway obediently, she called up to the first landing in a foreign language, maybe French, and I saw as she went up the stairs that she was a woman, not a girl. I went up behind the full curve of her hips, the dark skirt. Up she went fast and confident, blatant. I was speechless with admiration.

I sat on the bed and felt nothing, no desire, only a great gasping fear because I didn't know what to do and a gulping fearful excitement at doing something so forbidden, unspeakable, unimaginable. I was with a pro, a woman whose trade was with men below the belt: no shame, and what a relief that was, a woman smiling indulgently at the cock bulging in your trousers, the terrible fact transformed, no longer ugly. She was there to be blocked, the price was fixed, no arguments. Take it or leave it. And it was alright and you were grateful, the guilt ran out of you and you sat on the bed smiling and felt no desire, in some curious way it had got left outside the door with the top half, the part above the belt. You sat numbly, without feelings, just a swirl of fears and a stirring of shame because you'd paid and the woman was there ready, she was an expert, a professional, she had her pride. What the hell was wrong with you? Why were you such an insult?

She dropped a little shower of dirty pictures on the bed and left the room. My trousers were round my ankles, I sat looking at my bare legs and they looked foolish, helpless. I was half-hard, she came and sat beside me in her slip, stockings rolled down, heavy white thighs inert. She stroked me between my legs and I lay down on the bed and nothing happened and she said, still patient. 'Don't you have a sweetheart to do this for you?' Her words stuck in me like a thorn, bitter, sharp.

It must have been how she said it, the touch of amusement and the pity, or it may have been the dread of catching the pox. I sat up and started to cry. Then she was furious: her face shrivelled with rage. She stood up, dragging on clothes furiously and shouting 'Don't do that, don't be so stupid, stop that! I can't waste any more time, I've got somebody else waiting to use this room.' She disappeared, and a maid came to show me out, very polite, like a sedate waitress in a teashop.

'Will you pull the door shut at the bottom of the stairs, sir?'

I gave her a tip.

Outside in the street I was completely lost, I felt mad and emptied and lost, I wanted to run, to yell. The rain had stopped and the sky was ragged, trailing moonlight. With my head back I looked at the sky and ran, bursting with a desire to apologise, to ask forgiveness. I turned back and ran up and down the street searching for the green door and it was no good, I couldn't find it. Nothing looked the same; the whole thing was like a dream.

## 11

LONDON. Saturday in Nottingham a yawning pit to cross over, so one weekend I catch an excursion train, flee to London. The regal arches of the station are always exciting. The great threshold. The pomp of the capital awaits me. I leave the station purposefully, as if I'm going somewhere. Walk my legs off getting lost, keep going, catching the crowd fever, the million-footed tread. The rhythm drugs me, the pleasure of drowning in the sea of crowds, drugged by the amazing variety of faces, the richness of unknown lives, staring into faces, looking for God knows what. That's all I ever do in London.

Back to the station at midnight more dead than alive to sit exhausted among the dregs, the derelicts. Go underground into the stale air of the white-tiled cellars for a piss and nearly fall over a man, only young, dark round head and slender body, stretched out asleep on newspapers on the tiled floor, head pillowed on his arms.

No train for me until five to one. I go into the buffet and buy coffee and cake at the wet steely counter, sit at one of the round tables in the institution-like atmosphere that station eating places have, the woodwork heavy and dark, oppressive, the ceiling high and grimy, weary as an old yellowing biscuit, floor scummy and littered with the day's traffic, sloppings, spent matches, ash, crumbs, fag ends. Two of the tables occupied by silent engrossed couples, the rest vacant. Then I notice the old drunk slumped over a table at the back, he starts mumbling harmlessly to himself and I notice him. It's like a stage set; above him there's a grill giving a view of the pavement outside, feet and ankles going by occasionally. A policeman stoops down, looks in—obviously he's made a habit of peering in from up there. In a matter of seconds he's downstairs to the entrance and marching in, young, truculent bony jaw stuck out under his bucket helmet, slamming down his feet in an ominous manner as if he's leading in a regiment. He makes straight for the drunk and stands over him, bullish and planted, his face set.

'I told you before,' he says, 'and I shan't tell you again. Now get up.'

I watch over the rim of my cup, trying to imagine the crime the old man's committed. He sits mumbling to himself and whining, he hardly knows where he is. Then the Law has him by the arm, dragging him to his feet.

'Move,' the Law says loudly, even glaring angrily about to see who else he can tackle. I keep my eyes down, sickened, heart pumping black blood into all manner of crimes I'd love to commit.

'Did you hear me?' he bawls in the old man's ear. 'I don't want to see you in here again. So move!' The old man sways on his feet, hopelessly fuddled, hands pawing the air. He gets a violent shove in the small of his back to help him along, blunders forward in a rush off balance and goes down, sprawling between the tables. Infuriated, the Law bounds up and yanks him to his feet, bundles him out of the door with his jacket bunched up round his ears, shouting what he'll do to him next time. I give them time to get clear because I can't trust myself, twitching about on the chair, unable to sit there any longer. I want to rub London off the map, heave it out of my guts. The glittering vitality of its streets is a mirage. Somehow this scene has summed it all up; the gigantic proud engine of the city is full of ashes, cold ashes. It's a dustbin.

My train is still a good half hour away. I go and sit on the benches for waiting passengers under the big clock, on the platform in the open. Better than the waiting room, which is lugubrious, like a foyer to the underworld.

More slumped rejects scattered on the seats, snoozing, one

eye open for coppers. I'm glad to be sitting among them. Never more sure where I belong.

Farther along the same bench a well-dressed woman, small, middle-aged, is bent over sleeping, clutching tightly at her black shiny handbag. A kid of twenty in a pink shirt, grubby but with a fastidious air to him, comes up trailing a beefy young bloke in a dark suit who grins round at all and sundry good-naturedly.

'Christ Almighty, look at her,' nags Pinky, gazing down at the woman and tut-tutting. His pal sits down on one side of the woman and him on the other. They want to be together but there's no room, the woman's in the way. Pinky is close to me, his bleached curly hair wags censoriously over the unconscious woman.

'Isn't it disgusting?' he bleats to me, gives me a hard look. Close up he looks twitchy and drained, beaten.

'Is she drunk?'

'Yeh, oh yeh,' he says. Lighting a fag, his hand trembles. 'If it's one thing I can't bear to see it's a woman drunk in public. Bloody awful, it really is.' And he keeps wagging his head, agreeing with himself.

'You here for the night?' I ask him.

'Who, me?' he says warily, suddenly sharp. 'Oh yeh, yeh I am, that's right. Here for the night, actually. You?'

I tell him I'm waiting for the next train to Nottingham.

'Is that so? Go on. Nice place, Nottingham, oh yeh. Worked in a hotel there once, Black Boy is it? Ever heard of it?'

His eyes never still, his head twitching and wagging, and a large part of him absent when he talks, like a somnambulist. Fatigue is creeping through him but he shrugs it off, refuses to relax.

I ask him if he comes here most nights.

'Yeh, I do actually, as a matter of fact.' He puts a more pettish, acrimonious note into his voice, his eyes swivel over the platforms. 'Well it's like this, you see, I get sick and tired of paying two pounds a night at a hotel, it's such a bloody racket. Isn't it, really? I mean, you think: up at seven in the morning, swallow a cup of tea and out to work all day just to pay for your hotel, it's never worth it is it, really?'

I murmur sympathetically.

'Sick and tired of it I am, as a matter of fact.'

He sits musing, smoking, drifting off again.

'Don't blame you,' I say, thinking You're a liar, but if you want to put up a front it's all the same to me. 'I wouldn't pay those prices.'

'No, it's not the money,' he says quickly, 'it's the bloody principle of the thing. After all . . . Christ Almighty . . .'

'Yes, you're right,' I say, nodding now as regularly as him, catching the habit.

'You a Londoner?' I ask him.

'Me? No, Irish,' he says dreamily, like a man speaking of a place he can only dimly remember. 'Bray, outside Dublin...'

He reaches out and gives the sleeping woman a shake, spitefully.

'Wake up, Missus,' he says conversationally, 'the platform's going out.'

His pal laughs from the other side, watching, the woman unfolds, groans, opens her eyes painfully, croaks, 'No bleedin' peace,' and begins to sing, as she rolls to and fro and opens the clasp of her handbag, fumbles inside, fetches out a flat bottle in a crumpled paper bag and unscrews the cap.

'Oh my Christ,' mutters my friend. 'What have you got there, eh?'

And he leans his nose over, sniffs at the top of the bottle.

'I thought so,' he says, wrinkling his nose in disgust, the woman swigging away from the concealed bottle between snatches of song. 'Meths.'

He smokes and stares straight ahead, his body lifeless as a statue but his white face afflicted with nerve tremors, eyelids fluttering. He draws in his head, he's a bird of prey. His profile listens. 'Christ yes,' he says softly, as if to himself, 'and she's got another bottle of medicine in her handbag. See that? Two, she's got.'

He leans over the woman, nods with his long nose. 'I see you got another in there,' he says loudly.

She snatches her bag out of reach. '. . . . your own business . . .'

I get to my feet stiffly and go off for my train. 'So long—time I went.' Going, I wave at him.

'Is it really?' Pinky says, waking up to the fact of me now I'm going. 'Bye bye, old man,' nodding his farewell politely, watching me with mocking eyes.

## 12

BEFORE I met Lou and for a while afterwards I had a clerk's job out at Banstead, the huge ordnance depot on the edge of the city. I'd leave my bedsitter furtively, slip out past the closed doors like a burglar and get the bus at the bus station, feeling utterly nameless, nothing, as we went nosing out through the grimy brick channels. It was the first time I'd ever worked away from home, in a strange town. It was spring, it could have been any season.

I sit clutching my money: half-past seven or a bit later, shivering in the damp air, speechless, nothing but a busload of cargo. That *Modern Times* shot of them all funnelling into a factory in thousands, changing suddenly from people to sheep at a cattle market being herded between the steel fences—it's not like that when you're one of the herd. You sit on the bus as if alone, you nurse very carefully this gnawing emptiness as though the bottom has dropped out of life. It's you alone: the others might not exist. You shrink away from them, especially the veterans, the pipe-smokers, tough leathery grey-heads with impassive expressions who reinforce the general picture of normality—their set shoulders, the placid, regular puffs of smoke—and you want to bow your head like a man entering Dartmoor who is crushed by the sight of the walls, their thickness, worst of all their terrible permanence. The relentless forward thrust of the bus affects you: it'll never break down, never get lost. It doesn't, either. Drops you neatly outside the gates and still you have the choice. Everybody has. What carries you in on clockwork legs isn't the others, as it seems on the film, it's not the rising of the dead or the rush of the lemmings; no, everybody acts for himself. Everybody is convinced and crushed by the efficiency of the arrangements, the streets laid out symmetrically in a rigid pattern, the unhesitating bus on its cold timetable, aimed like a projectile for the gates, loaded and ready. You can't beat that: nothing is allowed to dawdle. Soon you don't even question it. Far easier not to. The system's fixed, immovable, vast, the structure you go threading through was in existence before you were born. Foundations all over the world, enormous girder-work sunk deep and set in the concrete of centuries. It'll last for ever . . . amen.

You rise with the others. Somewhere like a bomb ticking there's a woman planted: only a woman could make this lot crumble. In your dread you seize on that, weave fantasies, you rise with the dead and buried deep in you, secret, something frantic snatches at a bit of warmth and freshness. You go in.

I got to hear of the job because of the man downstairs who collected the rents and did odd jobs for the landlord, slopped out the rooms with green distemper as they came empty. Always the same colour. Grass green he called it, showing me my room, which had just had the treatment. I could smell it from the landing, dank, chemical.

'Fresh, en it,' he gobbled, swung his head round to admire his handiwork and then turned on me the kind of mirthless grimace that made you shiver. He was short, ferrety, bilious under the eyes; he gave me a resentful glare I couldn't comprehend when I asked for a front door key.

'You can have one if I got one. An' a rent book. I'll have a look.'

And shot out on the landing and down the stairs in a rickety scuttling movement, like a hunted man.

I followed him down. In his room on the ground floor facing out on the street he attacked the debris of clothes piled in heaps on the sideboard, muttering about the chaos and who's shifted his rent books, until his wife loomed out from the kitchen, hot-faced and suspicious, a big menacing figure.

She seemed a little confused by my presence and let the man rattle on, otherwise I don't think he'd have dared. He knew he was safe. 'How many times have I asked you not to move them books?' he moaned, still turning over socks and underpants, working himself up into a frenzy.

'Look on the mantelpiece,' the woman said flatly.

He turned on her, exasperated, mouth open, but the sourness and malevolence of the look she gave him was enough. He kept quiet until she'd left the room.

'Why don't you leave my bloody stuff alone, where I can find it,' he swore under his breath, darting about.

He gave me a rent book, and a key, and told me to watch out for the woman across the hall, whose husband was in the navy. 'Everybody who comes here seems to think she's a good grind, well I ent avin' it. This is a decent house.'

Then after a few days I heard about the job at the depot: he worked there himself. The first morning I went in with him. He had a small attaché case for his snack and thermos, and no sooner had we stepped inside the big gates past the police box than he shot forward, leaning forwards from the waist in a racing walk, then scurried off to the left up one of the side avenues. I remember how his chest suddenly stuck out and he nearly burst his collar with self-importance. Seven years he'd been there and I suppose he wanted to show it was his domain, his little kingdom. He was some sort of chargeman at one of the store counters: he had his morsel of power to give him that extra puff and strut.

It was an incredible place, a town, roads and intersections of its own, great hump-backed sheds crouched alongside railway tracks, some of them heaped to the roof girders with packing cases, others full of tanks and armoured cars, snub-nosed bulgy olive-green tin cans on wheels. For nearly a week I kept getting lost, then I located the barracks over to the north, in the upper field against the wire fence—I could get my bearings from that. You'd hear the 'come to the cookhouse' ta-ra on the bugle, and quite a bit of parading up and down. Later on I went wandering up closer and peered in at the paymaster's office—more clerks—and the guardroom, and once I saw a little posse of ramrods marching some poor sod in between the flowerbeds on a charge. 'Left . . . whee-al!' Ever since the war a recurring nightmare of mine has been the call-up, finding myself in a suit as thick as sacks, deep-sea diver boots and a number as long as the envelope on all my letters, wheeling and gasping with a swollen kitbag, at the mercy of these spit-and-polish bastards. So at first I crept about warily and kept my distance, afraid I might be sucked in even now: after all conscription was still going strong and I was young enough. Each time I found myself nearby I'd creep a little nearer, goggling at them, their town-in-a-town, kids of the young generation dwelling in that incredible comic opera land, playing goodies and baddies with real guns, bullets, bayonets . . . it was archaic, so funny, they kept spitting and polishing and frog-marching because they'd always done it: somebody had mislaid the order to halt. Still, it was frightening, it was still nightmarish when I saw those red necks and shaved skulls, that health, the mild English freshness of the National Service boys as they blundered about so willingly, so resigned. I found that it was the thrill of fear I got, coming up a bit closer and closer each time, which gave the pleasure. Then one Monday, in the corner of the big office where I sat keeping records of officers, the files stamped 'Private and Confidential', amending their details on the card index and the chart so we had an accurate personal record of each officer, his posting, rank, home address, etc, etc—up marched these two big-booted boys from Liverpool. They were National Service lads, drafted in for a spell of clerical work, though there was bugger-all to give them. They sat at the tables and nodded at me, and one gave me a huge wink.

'Cushy number, this,' he said. He was Curly, he explained, and his mate was called Jacko.

I carried on working and kept sizing him up, this Curly, the one who impressed me. I was slightly elated at the idea of some new company, and I liked the glint of devilment in his eye. He had a gamin quality, I could imagine him dodging through a warren of decrepit back streets, giving orders, a gang leader. The army hadn't got him; nothing had. He knew how to slip under fences, gazes, from tight corners. And get a kick out of doing it.

My boss was a fierce lip-biting ex-serviceman with an artificial leg and a medal, quick as a terrier, very proud of the efficiency of his tiny section. We ran it between the two of us and had time to spare, he'd go limping all over the building poking his nose into other people's affairs, I'd hear his thin yelping laugh and glance across and there he was, jabbing somebody in the chest, waving his arms about. Back stiff, collar and tie immaculate, ready for inspection, not a hair out of place. His colleagues admired him for his energy, courage, high spirits. Now he saw the two young soldiers arrive, spotted them from a distance and came stumping over, rubbing his hands briskly: he was delighted to have a little squad of his own again, like old times.

'Alright, lads, let's be having you—now this is the drill,' he barked, and they stopped slouching in their chairs and sat up stiff, startled for a minute or two, till they got his number. No work to give them, so he set them busy repairing the most tatty-looking files, replacing the covers of the worst ones. He could never stay still: in five minutes he was away again, off to the far side of the vast room. But if an officer breezed up with some query or other, or to register his arrival, you could bet Maurice would be on the spot before he left again, breathing down the man's neck: 'Everything satisfactory, sir? Any further information you may require, sir, let us know and we'll soon have it chased up—okay, sir?' He threw in plenty of sirs but looked them straight in the eye and never sucked up to them. More than once I saw one of the young, rather languid subalterns flinch and go pink, backing away from his head-on attacks.

Curly was a heavy hulking lad, ginger; when he sat down he planted his elbows on the table the way his boots were on the floor. He existed, he was a fact, like his meaty hands. When he said something funny he opened his eyes wide and kept his face deadpan: his humour was pure Scouse. Maurice took to him, I could see how it was going to be. He liked his independence, he recognised a kindred spirit. The other lad, Jacko, was too shadowy to bother anybody or be noticed hardly, a dark scrannel with a pasty pimply face and a red mouth which struck you as shocking, it was so lurid, and swollen and sore like a blister. He had nothing to say; he lived in the shadow of the other one.

Soon it was full summer and I still stuck there, mainly from inertia. I was in a trance, what with the strange city, knowing nobody, my affair with Leila stagnant. She'd gone to Norfolk with her family and some friends, nothing to do with me. I'd met Lou but hadn't been to his place or got thick with him. At the depot there was even less work to do, long yawning afternoons when I stepped out for a breather on the tarmac runways and found myself drifting between the sheds, a haze of heat on the turf and flowers over towards the barracks. Then I'd go back inside and sit down in the corner and nobody had missed me: I was like the invisible man. The warehouse job all over again, I thought, except that here you didn't have to pretend, if you weren't busy you cleared off outside. It didn't matter, as long as someone was there holding the fort for any officer who shot in with his case history. But the supply of officers seemed to dry up with the coming of the hot weather. Maurice dodged out of sight more often, and once I was wandering round a corner near the sidings and bumped into Curly and Jacko, both of them strolling along nice and easy but purposeful, as if they were really going somewhere.

'Eh, I thought you was holding the fort, wack,' Curly said, stopping dead in his tracks like a cowboy and giving me his look. The blue-eyed boy.

'I thought *you* were,' I said.

We stood having a quiet laugh and Jacko's eyes kept slithering about warily, keeping a lookout. They were in uniform, conspicuous. Curly seemed indifferent, but he was nobody's fool: you could never tell what he was thinking.

'Good ole Maurice,' Curly said. 'Hope he ain't too lonely.'

'If he's there,' I said.

'See you then, me ole fruit,' Curly said, moving off.

'Where you going?' I called.

'Nowhere,' he said, 'same as you. See who gets there first.'

'See how far it is.'

'Tarra,' he said, waving.

# 13

A LETTER from Ray caught me by surprise, struck into me fiercely: walking around the streets of this city had bitten through the cord of our closeness and I thought we were lost to each other. There was his gabby scrawl and I loved to see it. I tore open the envelope joyfully, unsuspecting, and the letter overwhelmed me with the force of its longing, too vivid, too much. It struck at me, sharp and soft at once, his real tongue, the dedicated desperation I knew better than my own, it slid down my throat and made my eyes smart, burst deep inside me with a warm explosion. And left me stranded in a heap of darkness, a kind of thick vapour of loneliness, my heart thawed to no purpose. It wasn't letters I wanted, it was him in the room, standing there before me: timid and ineffectual in the eyes of the world, bold and decisive to me. Now more than ever I wanted him in the flesh, to feast my eyes on, now his presence haunted the grubby room.

'I'm in the park, Thursday, it's my dinner hour. In the park with the phoenix, who sits beside me consummated with a cheese sandwich. A few yards away there's a cat with a gleeful expression. I have to report many clouds, they hove in sight from all directions. The sun still sweeps through them. It's not really a park here but just a grove with a lot of trees, off the Parade, remember? In the heart of the town with sounds of traffic rumbling all around I always think of those parks in London with their strange sanctuary quiet and the city roar tucked away, hidden. Or even of the churchyard in the middle of Brum. Bell chimes—half past one. You know this dance routine upside down! A young chap on this bench has just told me it's his first day at work. He's in his Sunday best, poor bugger. An office. Getting used to it now, he says. A businessman in a brown summer suit has perched between us. Polishes his specs, the paper is unfurled. REDS REPLY: LET'S TALK. I sneak another squint: "Last woman left tells her story." He's moved now. The kid gets up and goes as well. Businessman on the grass in the shade, the sun's too strong for him. It's nearly as strong as I am—stop shoving, sun.

'Evening now, the prison gates opened with a clang and I went streaking off down Union Street like a mad horse just escaped from the circus. Tonight the horizon is more naked than I've ever seen it, the sea a very deep dark blue, and to look at the horizon pushes your eyes back into your head, snap, it's so close, it's all there is and you can tell there's a hell of a drop beyond it where the sea's pouring over in a vast silent waterfall. The horizon moves in even closer—comes to have a look at us all: the far headland seems beyond the horizon, clear and shining in the setting sun . . .

'I wonder if you remember how the evening sun lights up this cottage room? Our paintings are still up on the walls, the salt air rusts the drawing pins. The wireless is hidden in the corner by the window, the heather is still in the vase, the sea still outside the door.

'Whenever I look ahead into the future—and it must be the same for you—I can't reach forward more than a few months without wondering where I'll be. What a state of affairs! While I live this treadmill routine it's a twisted sort of consolation to know that *some* change is inevitable at short notice, yet how I dream of a time, a place, which all the weathers nourish, and each day grows out of the one before in a natural ritual, and me part of it, in it, instead of gnawing away at the skirting boards like dry rot, like a rat on the fringes, wishing my bloody life away . . . Like you when you worked here, I dive down to the office lav for some privacy now and then. My hermit's cell. It stinks too, this one. The green mould on the window ledge is growing luxuriant, looks like a lush meadow a long way off. The smashed window with the wire netting outside, the council flats, the black grimed windows that won't open. Enough, I've had enough. Can't go on like this any longer, hanging on the brink. For months I've been stoked with this feeling, of being on the point of making a great break. Every day my veins choke with rage, the storms pour through me. My guts are sown with dynamite, one day I'll go off with an almighty bang. I seem to be walking about half the time with my eyes closed and a great light sizzling through my eyelids. What's happening to me? How long can it last like this?

'Another day, Friday: this is a continuous performance. I'm sitting in a stationary train at the station, en route to a creek near Saltash—we've heard of this motor torpedo boat and we might rent it. It's been moored up permanently and converted to a houseboat, 32/6 a week including barnacles. I remember how I used to look at the station here at North Road with such tenderness, go and stand near it, because when I was doing my National Service it meant freedom to me. This very station would bring a lump in my throat, just thinking of it. Once I was wandering round the town all evening with a book in my hand—Fyodor—and found myself outside the station. Dark and drizzling. Went into the wooden waiting room and there were some old folk in there wheezing with age and some kids shouting. It was dimly lit, raining outside and Prince Myshkin had just thrown a fit, a fit of such beatitude that I was spellbound, I wanted to foam at the mouth and be as blessed . . . Train's moving, here we go, first stop Paradise—no it ain't, it's the dockyard halt. The dockyardies pile in, dozens of men, grim stone-faced bastards some of 'em, they fill the train like a tide and we go clanking off again, groaning and work-weary . . .

'Imagine us living on a boat, eh Colin? Twas on the good ship Venus—by God you should have seen us! Sail at daybreak, cast off at sunrise for the promised land, the Virgin

Isles, Cape of Good Hope, the Easter Islands, Samoa, Golden Bay, the Aegean, Land of Heart's Desire. Only one thing wrong, matey: what are all these ugly mugs I'm surrounded with?

'Those were the days be Jesus when we were mad comrades laughing fit to bust, making the roof ring, the gates of doom crack open—nothing mattered, we'd be staggering drunk with laughter on neat nothing. Let's have another binge old friend, I'm badly in need of some more of that intoxicating juice we distilled and shared. All I've done by way of affirmation since you left is one hand-sized watercolour, also put brake blocks on the bike and had a bath. Connie's thoroughly down in the mouth and who can blame her—I've been in the salt mines so long I've forgotten what my name is. Yes Colin if you do hitch down here for a few days this summer, that would be great. If we had one I'd put the red carpet out—the sea's already soaping itself all over, getting clean and ready. I'll have the laugh-drink brewed and bottled and be pacing up and down on the corner like a hoodlum waiting for his best cracked pal, long-lost twin, of the cracked order of champion chokers. So take care and be happy, never forget those times of ours.'

# 14

BEFORE I moved into the bedsitter I lived in a family house out at Sneinton, a grim district near the public baths. Once a week there was a market in the streets nearby, pushcarts appeared loaded with junk, old clothes, bedsteads, one or two lorries heaped with gaudy fabrics, lino, glassware, a man on the tailboard talking nonstop, a lump of wood in his fist for thumping on the rolls of lino. As a kid I was fascinated by their spiel and the way it ran out of their mouths seamless like the yards of flaming orange ribbon and lassoed us, bunched us into a captive crowd. One sharpie at Sneinton would give away free ball-pens with every purchase, he'd hand down a paper bag to his assistant after dropping in the article and then the pen very fastidiously from his finger and thumb: 'One, two for the price of one, it's ridiculous... another over there, and another, another!'

I was a lodger in a house with students, a bus driver, a young ex-miner. The Y.M. had given me the woman's address, and the day I tapped on the door she was getting a room ready for the students, she said. Really she was full up, she explained, but if I'd like to sit down a minute and excuse the mess she'd have another think, see if she could fit me in.

I took it that she had already decided, but liked to give the impression she was bestowing favours: a peculiarity of landladies.

We were at the rear of the house. Through the window I could see a narrow yard with a shed at the end. She saw me looking and said yes, she had another folding bed in there, that wasn't the problem, it was space she was stuck for. She was middle-aged, a tall floppy woman in a grey dress and slippers, wearing glasses. The glasses made her look shrewd and capable, then she took them off and I saw she was ignorant and cunning, her eyes a bit scatty and bloodshot.

'Don't let me put you to any trouble,' I said.

In those days I was perfectly willing to let a situation decide things for me. It wasn't fatalism, it was a kind of suspension of the will. If a thing pushed me in a certain direction, I went. At the back of it was I think the old nagging desire for something to happen. Perhaps this was the direction, now, so I went.

'It's a funny old life, don't you think?' the woman said, not even listening. Or so I thought. In fact she chose to ignore anything she didn't want to hear, but she didn't miss a thing.

'Now let's see what we can do about you, young man,' she said archly.

She was smirking and showing her dentures. Her voice was honeyed and crude and genteel, she slid from one to the other in the course of a single sentence. I shifted my feet uneasily as she gave me a hard unwavering look.

'What did you say your name was?'

I blushed because she wanted to know much more than that. I began to hate her. She had a queer nervous gobbling curiosity.

I told her.

'May I call you Colin?' she said, and now her eyes were ingratiating, she waited almost breathlessly and it was clear that a lot depended on how I answered.

'Certainly,' I said.

This had the effect of jerking her into action: from being a slovenly torpid creature she changed immediately, leapt up and bustled me out through the kitchen to help her bring in another bed.

'If you don't mind helping, that is,' she panted, dragging open the shed door and standing a moment in pretended horror: 'My son's been here again, I've told him a hundred times not to play here. Did you ever see anything like it?'

I stared in at the chaos, the cheap wardrobe, burst mattress, cobwebby pushbike with inner tube dangling, dark green cast-iron mangle, brass fenders, it was like market day all over again. But you're a liar to act surprised, I thought. The room I'd been sitting in was in absolute disorder and so was the kitchen: if I'd had to cook a meal in that mess I'd have been sick before I got to eating it. Funny, I wrinkled up my nose at the mingled gas and fried onion smells, the congealed fat on the cooker, sink jammed with dirty crocks, hurried through with my guts cringing in revulsion and yet it never occurred to me that I was contemplating living here, being fed from this filthy hole.

It turned out that the bed I was helping her carry was for the second student she'd taken on. It was an attic room at the back, with a view of the yards, sheds, wash-houses.

'Michael he's called. He's ever so nice, black curly hair like a golliwog, only small he is but full of cheek, in a pleasant way I mean, nothing offensive at all. And he's so cuddly, I'll have to be careful not to mother him. Still, some like to be mothered, don't they?'

I ended up that first night sharing a bed with Len, the ex-miner, a temporary arrangement while she retrieved more sheets from the laundry—'I'm sure that's where they are.' It was a three-quarter bed, stuck under the sloping ceiling in an even smaller attic room next-door to the students: I could hear them horsing around in there, cries of mock pain, snatches of false contralto. The radio came on, a news bulletin. Someone sliced off the voice in the middle of a flood disaster.

I got into bed and Len was already in, turned to the wall, his bare white arms looking big and significant on top of the blanket. Getting in I saw more of him. His singlet was too large; there was hair round his nipples. He was a young

Yorkshireman, disabled, so the landlady said, though he looked alright to me. Round baby face, moony white, his hair dank and pale, and his voice came out thick, slow, heavy and puzzled. Len Bolton.

It was the first time I'd slept with a complete stranger and it was curious how easy it was. We had no option, but all the same it could have been nasty. I didn't mind his stale, old-iron body smell. After all it was his bed, I was the intruder. We managed not to touch. To strike up some sort of aquaintanceship I asked him a few things and he answered shyly, obediently, like a timid kid replying to his teacher. I felt a fool, and guilty, as if I was probing. He was content to just lie there, stranger or not; it was all one to him.

'You say you haven't been in the Midlands long?' I said.

'About three yeer. Summat like that.'

'At Nottingham?'

'Ay, outside like. Moreton Wood pit, mostly. That was where I copped it.'

'Like it there, did you? Until the accident, I mean.'

'After a bit it weren't bad. Funny lot they are. I mean they're all right but they kept to themselves. Moreton gang wouldn't mix with them that cum from town, not at any price.'

'How about you, from Yorkshire?'

'Oh, they both gev it me, they did. I got ragged be both lots.'

'You got used to it, I suppose.'

'Oh ah.'

It wasn't quite dark, the man's breath came loud and regular beside me, the night thickening and moving in a respiration of its own and we sank slowly into it together. What light there was came from a street lamp outside.

I ought to have left him alone and it was clear I would have to, soon: he wasn't going to sleep but his silence was growing implacable. One thing kept nagging at me and I wanted his reaction.

'How d'you get on with the Mrs here?' I said.

Once again the response was immediate. He swung his body over to lie on his back and then waited inert like a discarded sack, cleared his throat portentously and I thought, Here we go—expecting a speech. But all he said was, 'She ent bad when she likes.'

Coming from him, the touch of animation was like a little explosion.

'When she likes?' I coaxed him.

'Ar, that's it.'

I laughed softly into the dark.

'What about when she doesn't?'

I thought he wasn't going to answer, that he was finished, but he gave one final burst before rolling over to face the wall again: 'Her, she's a bloody nuisance! Won't let yer alone . . . pesters yer to death . . .'

I had to sleep on that, but in the next few days I began to see what he meant. She blew hot and cold, blustery and coy by turns, hanging round the table when Michael the new student was having his breakfast. He was the present favourite. She'd done a stint with the bus driver, so I heard, going out drinking with him at night. I don't know what had gone wrong but he made himself scarce now, and when he did appear for a bit of tea some evenings she gave him the cold shoulder, spoke curtly, made her eyes anonymous, shoving across the pot of jam or whatever it was with a jab like a rebuff. I was intimidated as much as him. He took it without a word, stuffing his mouth and keeping his head down, especially if the husband was at the table. It was a queer atmosphere at that place: something was always going on. I soon learnt to mind my own business like the others. You had to keep your eyes to yourself, and make sure the friendliness was out of them if you looked: she was a great one for seizing on crumbs of encouragement. Sid, the husband, was a seething, acrid, thickset little man. If he did squeeze you out a smile it was sickly and measured like an undertaker's, and he had the face to go with it, cadaverous, droopy-nosed. He was a Derby man, with their flat working-day accent, and had the knack of repeating your question so that it sounded sarcastic, though it was probably habit.

Once on an impulse of pity I said, 'How are you?' and he snapped back as if it was red-hot, 'How am I? I'm as you see me, lad.' You're no great shakes then, I thought, and gave up even pretending to like him. He came in from his Co-op counter job each night and stalked through to the kitchen to inspect the squalor, which never altered all the time I was there. Back into the dining-room with his little-man strut. The yellow-faced glare he wore would be a picture, and completely lost on his wife. Tom, the other student, who seemed more or less a fixture amid the comings and goings of lodgers, could hit off Sid's tired whiney voice perfectly. 'Doris, can't you please get that kitchen a bit straight?' he'd mimic, up in his room.

They had two boys still at school, and because nobody cared what they did and their parents were always missing in the evenings, they ran riot whenever they were left alone. So the lodgers pushed off into town or the nearest pub for a bit of peace, the students likewise, if they weren't barricaded in their room and supposed to be studying, with the radio on full blast. Meeting them on the stairs they'd con me with dazzling smiles; they were as bland as the cream surfaces of the doors.

I'd have the evening meal to get my money's worth and then turn out with the others into the streets, waiting for the trolley bus or walking, all going in our different directions. It was like living at the Salvation Army. You'd munch up your grub mechanically and escape, quick, no idea where you were heading.

# 15

I CAN'T remember how I came to get hold of the address of the International Friendship League, the secretary, but it must have been while I was at Doris's. One evening I stood ringing at the door of a tall house in Elm Drive, close to the base of the Castle. The last thing I am is a joiner, but nothing was happening with Leila, I was well and truly lost in the void, and now I came on this ravishing word friendship. In the state I was in, weak with self-pity, it was irresistible. The very thought of it made my eyes prickle. I would have joined a bible class if someone had asked me nicely. Friendship: the sound it made in my head was like the password of a secret society. It would unlock the orchards, fields, the secret fruits. Open the cage. I wasn't bothered about the international part, it could be universal, provincial, spatial for all I cared. And I was on the track of it, I found myself in Elm Drive. I rang the bell. No answer. Rang. I could hear the ringing in the depths of the house. Someone came down the stairs.

The secretary was a Scotsman, a thin thoughtful fellow in his thirties, sucking a pipe. He looked too ordinary to be a dispenser of friendship. Up we went to his flat, a large high-ceilinged room with thick plaster mouldings and huge skirting boards, cream woodwork and olive green walls. I gazed in wonder at the shelves of books while he sat me down against the window and sat with crossed legs in a carved chair yards away, giving times of meetings, particulars of activities and so on. I listened to him vaguely, he was a teacher, telling me precisely but remotely what he thought I wanted to know, as if he had a whole group of people in front of him. His platitudinous nature rejected me of its own accord, without him even being aware of it. There was the urge to say: 'Go on talking if you like, but we're wasting our time.' The bell rang again and some friends came up, I sat for an hour or more on the fringe of things, content to absorb the air of leisure, the secretary's accent, which sounded exotic and fascinating. I enjoyed watching the working of his jaw.

'Would you care for a coffee?'

He smiled in an effort to include me.

'Thanks a lot,' I said, 'but I'd better be going.'

'Oh and if you're ever at a loose end at weekends,' he said rapidly, 'why don't you call on Mrs Collis, she keeps a sort of open house—I'm sure she'd be pleased to see you. Hang on, I'll write down the address. You know the Mansfield Road? It's out in that direction, past the Forest...'

Mrs Collis was the treasurer, another official. I called one summer evening, much later, after going to one session of the club and not having the stomach for another try. Still, I had the address and it was a private house, after all. It might be worth a visit, I said doubtfully in my mind.

The house was bigger than the one the secretary lived in: up a wide deserted side road with old-established chestnut trees growing out of the pavements. No voices: the kids of the district were either locked up or exterminated, I thought, forgetting that they were probably at boarding schools. All I could hear were wood pigeons cooing, a motor mower chugging in the depths behind one of the high keep-out walls. The one I wanted was called Beechwood, with a thick scratchy beech hedge sprouting out of a stone earth-filled wall at the front. I crunched over the gravel in the shade of wistaria and the coiled springs of a monkey-puzzle tree, the biggest I'd seen. Stone urns, roses, herringbone brick pathways, rings of turf crammed with begonias, the walls covered in ivy: everything was mellow and ordered. You felt constrained to walk sedately, appreciatively. It was a Saturday afternoon, dry and still. Two steps inside the gate and the city was cunningly spirited away. Not for a miniature landscaped country, no, it was a cloistered, monkish world the seclusion created. The door was at the side. It was what my mother would have called without resentment a posh house, simply meaning that the people who lived in such places were incomprehensible to her. To live surrounded by space, unused rooms and gardens laid out in a kind of pomp like a park was inhuman, even frightening. Such people must be terribly different, coldly so: she heard their loud confident voices and knew she was right. The money had made them hard, icy. Their big unfriendly houses were the same, they had to be. Beautiful, yes, but stately, stiffly beautiful. A cold beauty. She preferred small buildings, like cottages. They were human, they fitted you, snug and warm like a glove, stiflingly close so you were never alone and nothing echoed. In the posh houses of the wealthy she imagined Gothic horrors, cobwebs out of reach in high draughty corners, mad blazing cats and gloomy panelling, with peremptory voices everywhere, the voices of doctors, schoolmasters, solicitors, all the professional voices she dreaded.

They must have seen me approaching. As I reached the door it opened and a pretty girl with a pale high forehead, hurt mouth and thick long Alice-in-Wonderland hair stood waiting to welcome me. Unprepared, I began to stutter who I was.

'Do come in,' the girl said, cutting me short, and moving to one side she stood there, smiling. She seemed delighted to see me and I walked in gladly but I thought, How can she be, she's never set eyes on me before. Of course it was manners.

From behind she directed me like someone important into a large gracious room that was cool and restful, softly seductive with its velvet cushions and footstools, gold damask curtains in still waterfalls from ceiling to floor, brown embossed wallpaper in a Florentine design. Over by the French windows sat her mother, smoking a cigarette, examining a piece of embroidery; against her a sewing basket on legs. She nodded pleasantly to me and put her cigarette in an ash tray, but held on to the embroidery while she foraged in the sewing basket with her free hand.

'I'm Mrs Collis,' she said. 'Won't you sit down, Mr Patten?'

'Thanks very much,' I said. I glanced round for the girl but she'd slid away.

'That was Amanda,' Mrs Collis said, moving her legs. A long skinny woman, beaky, hair drawn back severely, flat on her head like a black shiny cap, parted exactly in the middle. 'She's the youngest. I have another daughter at university, Sarah, and a son, Quentin, who's married and lives in Kenya.'

'And a dog,' I said, seizing my chance. A silky fawn Peke, no bigger than a cat, had jumped down from a stool and come prancing up, jaunty and comical on its short bandy legs, to put its flat nose-holes against the toe of my shoe. It stayed there, eating the scent. I put my hand down to it and it collapsed sideways against my leg, eyes bulbous, showing the whites, and there was its tender studded belly on show, abandoned, soft and pinkish like a piglet's.

'Oh yes, that's Ching,' said Mrs Collis, her mouth lifted at one side in a crimped smile of appreciation. 'There's another one somewhere.'

'Smallest I've seen,' I said.

'She is tiny, isn't she? I think they call them sleeve pigs.'

'I haven't heard of that.'

'Oh yes. They're a Chinese dog, you know; Imperial China, of course. A court dog.'

I nodded, though I hadn't known. The long string of pearls hanging down into her lap struck me as incongruous. I was half listening to her and also absorbing the room, its untidiness, which had to do with leisure and money and carelessness, a cool attitude to living, asking nobody's approval. With the poor, tidiness was a necessity. Her domain was impressive, yet I didn't believe in any of it, or the liberal values that went with it. In my mind I took it like a toy and twirled it by the corners: I bristled with dissent. This room, the civilised woman being kind to me—it was a package licked all over with the safe, sheltered life these folk sucked in at their mother's breasts. Or was that done any more? Surely as a breed they managed to get their kids weaned without suffering the humiliation of that disgusting part? Even the welcome I was getting was suspect, somehow cancelled at the outset by the cool air of disengagement. My mother would have been strained and peculiar, anxious and flustered if she had to entertain someone she didn't like, bustling and eager if she liked them. Either way you'd soon know, there'd be no doubt. Here it was all manners, principles, nothing registered on the feelings. This left you free to be yourself, respected your thoughts, opinions, an ear listening most cordially to anything you might say, but emotions ran thin and you had a sneaking feeling they were unmentionable; at the very least they were messy, avoidable. Just as sex was unacknowledged in my mother's world, a nasty fact you could skate around by ignoring, hoping it would go away. Except at night, you could let it out then, under the sheets and private where it belonged. But feelings, she was lapped around with them in her family and all her activities. Thoughts were of no account, just words. Feelings were inescapable, hot waves of exchange between people, pressing away, pulling in. Her breast ached with the rich emotional charge, her memory a dark turgid compost. They wore her out, and it was impossible to bypass them in her mind, stand outside herself in a thought, an idea, even for a moment's respite. Work and feelings went pouring like a warm snake through the days of her life, filling her world completely, right to the corners.

And as long as I lived with her I was the same: not pawed over, hugged and kissed, we were an undemonstrative, reticent family, but swaddled by her constant loving devotion, nevertheless. She couldn't help herself. As a boy I exploited her love shamelessly, took and took and gave nothing in return. She asked nothing, never once complained, the joy for her was all in the giving. It was when I grew restless, itched to be off, started shutting myself away in my room—that made her bite her lip and want to cry out. I can think of some utterly contented mother-and-son times which must have been the happiest days of her life, wandering through the market with her on school holidays when we had little shared jokes, say a woman bearing down on us placidly with vast shaking bosom and I'd whisper from the side of my mouth, 'Jelly on a plate'. She pretended to be shocked, said, 'Colin!' and then blushed and laughed like a girl. The man on the stall where they sold sheets, plaid tablecloths, napkins, thick yellowish working men's vests and long pants, he sang out loud and guttural whenever the searching women delved too freely, 'Nah then ladies, if yer don't want the goods don't maul 'em!' and this was a war cry we mimicked and were always repeating, to amuse each other. 'Don't maul 'em, don't maul 'em!'

In those market forays I made a beeline for the magazine counter, we brought a pile of comics from the house for my mother to trade in: I forget how much he allowed us but it was useful and I came away with a fresh batch, *Hotspurs* and *Rovers* and *Skippers*, never the *Magnet* or *Gem* or *Boys' Own*. They were secondhand, dog-eared, but to me they were glowing with unread adventures. My mother paid the man carefully from her purse, the black purse she gripped like a lifeline, and rearranged her shopping basket to make room for the wad of magazines. From that moment the basket had an effulgence. She said, 'There, that'll keep you out of mischief for an hour or two' and we were on our way home, arms linked like old lovers. Passing near the fish counters she'd say, 'Do you fancy some haddock for tea? Would you like that?' and I answered off-hand, grudgingly, 'Don't mind.'

Or more than likely I said, fussy as an old maid, 'If it's not too salty.' She knew how I finicked over my food and she liked to pander to me, asking me to try this or that but often spoiling me, giving in to my whims and fancies. Not my father. The waste on my plate would disgust him, he'd snarl, 'Make him eat it,' and 'If he can't finish that dinner, don't give him any pudding, he's not hungry.' But where meals were concerned my mother ruled, on came the pudding, steaming with newness, and I got a helping like the others. My father tucked into his with relish and forgot me, rattling away with his spoon vigorously, chasing the last gobbet of custard.

# 16

'WOULD YOU like to go through to the garden?' Mrs Collis was saying, honeyed and vague, receding further each time she opened her mouth.

She was a good sort, I suppose. All the same I didn't need any encouragement to leave. The unreality was becoming a strain: the blue grass of the carpet was sapping my energy. The grit and grind of the streets were beginning to seem very desirable.

Out in the garden Amanda was sitting in a deck chair reading, and on one of those suspended garden seats with striped upholstery and an awning sat a youth, he could have been her boy friend, idly pushing himself to and fro with his foot. Seeing me approach he put the brake on at once and smiled, perfectly friendly and in charge of himself, a friendliness very much aware of the vulgarity of overflowing. I lowered my backside into the carnival upholstery, feeling stupid to be posed there on the gay colours like an advertisement. It was comfortable alright. I sank back discreetly in the corner.

'This is nice,' I said, for something to say.

'Isn't it,' the brown-haired youth said.

Half an hour dozed by and I couldn't see the point, I was about to get up and say cheerio when Mrs Collis appeared with a wicker tray, glasses of orange squash. It was getting on for five before I decided to make a break for it.

'Call in again whenever you're passing, won't you,' Mrs Collis droned out absently, and her daughter glanced up from her book and gave me such a warm smile, exactly like the one she'd doled out at the door, clapping eyes on me for the first time. Out in the street and making for the main road into the centre, the jubilation and rumpus of a city Saturday night, I let out a huge sigh of relief, relaxing. My blood ran free, I was alone and glad in my skin. Being lonely wasn't so bad after all. I strode along loose and irresponsible like a vagabond, whistling like a blackbird, cheerfulness spurting out of me at every step. I knew I wouldn't be back there again.

But I did land up at a house not far from there, later. I'd gone once with Aline because the woman was a friend of hers and she wanted me to meet her: this friend had a strange niece who was a bit mad and might have a touch of genius, Aline thought. She wrote poems on a blackboard and they got rubbed off in the course of time and lost forever. Her aunt encouraged her, let her do whatever came into her head within limits, even though she was baffled by the girl's behaviour.

'What about her parents, what do they think?' I asked.

'She hasn't got any,' Aline said. 'They were killed in the war.'

The girl wasn't in when we called, but we sat having tea and scones in the drawing-room, and bang in the middle of the carpet, before the window, was an easel and blackboard, half the size of a school one, and three verses of a poem scrawled over it, untitled, filling up all the space. I couldn't decipher many of the words, but Marion, the aunt, didn't seem concerned about the content, it was the activity, the phenomenon, she found extraordinary. She was a short puggy intense woman; crisp greying hair and a bright, happy voice, and I tried to imagine what her niece was like. Marion kept talking, referring to her niece in an attitude of complete acceptance, passing no judgements. Only in her eyes could you detect the mother signs, the lurking apprehension. She had no children of her own. 'She's a remarkable woman,' Aline had said. 'Betty's lucky to have an aunt like her.' She was unusual, certainly, but I didn't know where I was with her. It struck me as a funny set-up and I began to feel sorry for the girl, whatever she was like. Maybe she would have been better off with a demanding mother, I thought.

The blackboard stood and stared at us from the middle of the room, so bloody significant you had to look back at it and comment on it.

'Did she write that long ago?' I said.

'Oh no, only yesterday.'

'She doesn't just write poems, does she?' Aline said, prompting, wanting me to have the full story.

'No she doesn't, she often does drawings.'

'What of?' I said.

'Trees, always trees.'

I decided to shut up, it was somehow ridiculous, we were sitting around all solemn and ponderous like a bunch of trick cyclists.

The next time I was there alone, a spasm of curiosity had got me there and this time the girl was at home. No resemblance to her aunt: a tall thin gawk, cloud of long black hair tied with a red ribbon, straight bony nose that gave her a puritanical look. She was dressed wrong for her age. She wore white ankle socks and a drab pleated skirt, a queer mixture of too young and too old. She stared at me haughtily and refused to speak, gliding soundlessly out of the room as soon as she could. Her timidity was hard and lacquered, it wore a shell of arrogance, something I knew all about. In the drawing-room the first thing I noticed was the blackboard, it was wiped clean.

To my amazement Marion started talking to me in a detached yet curiously urgent manner, questioning me about my relationship with Aline. Finally she said quietly, smiling and steady, 'You know she's married, don't you?'

Resistance stiffening at once, I said, 'Separated.'

'Yes but Francis is hoping they'll come together again, he wants it very much.'

I blurted out stupidly, 'Who's Francis?' and could have bitten my tongue off. Now she had the whip hand.

She maintained her neutral role with her lips, smiling calmly, while her eyes said clearly: Now why don't you run along and stop being a nuisance, like a good little boy.

'Does *she* want it?' I said, stubborn, slipping down the slope and digging in my fingers, demoralised and cornered by the swift attack. The treachery of it dazed me, I felt sick and guilty. The woman saw my defencelessness and pressed in, triumphant.

'Oh I'm sure she does in her heart of hearts,' she said, superbly confident and knowing, and her voice expressed the deep concern of a friend. I sensed that its resonance was meant to shame me. 'You don't know her, she has such tremendous pride—that's the whole crux of the problem.' She paused, showed at last the cold steel of her hostility, her face shutting me out for good. 'If you care for her, I shouldn't keep on seeing her. You're making things worse for her, I'm sure you can see that. We musn't be selfish, must we?' And the mask was back, she was actually laughing, showing me to the door.

'Will you think about what I've said?' she purred smoothly.

'Sorry,' I said, walking off stiff-legged with hate for her, the advice gathering inside me like a poison, seething. Sorry, sorry, I was yelling inside, furious at the deception, the sprung trap, the oiled ease and unruffled calm of it. Everything in the garden was always lovely for these well-layered bastards, they never dirtied the air with foul language, screamed blue murder, came at you with a broken bottle, they just smiled like a dear friend as they slid the knife in and said ta-ta. Well she could take a running jump, I wasn't even listening, I was a thousand miles away, I was as deaf as my grandfather. Sorry, you rotten bitch, sorry and get stuffed, sorry for nothing you smirking shit. I was afraid now, I imagined enemies everywhere. Worse still, I had the worm of doubt wriggling through me, those words she'd dropped into my ear so sweetly had taken on a life of their own. And perhaps she was right. Who was telling the truth, who could I trust? I even doubted her, Aline. I pushed along in a fury of hurt pride and fear, squirming again and again in that boxed-in corner, turning my head to avoid the advice like a betrayer, like a man trying to ward off the truth, the slap in the face. What I was most scared of was the sudden terrifying challenge without warning to my own powers. I wouldn't admit this to myself but it was true: I just didn't know how strong I was. That was what was being tested, the strength or weakness of my desire. In a wild instinct of self-preservation I kept laying into the woman, the advice-giver, all the way into town.

# 17

FOR NEARLY a week I had Lou's address and did nothing about it, though my instinct was to go straight there and knock on his door. I stored him up, kept him for a rainy day, tasted the pleasures of denial. He was a contact, a friendly face. The instant I got back to the bedsitter, climbed the stairs past the navy man's wife screaming at one of her kids behind the door, unlocked the padlock on my own door and went in, I thought of Lou Coltman. His address was burning a hole in my pocket but I still hung back, unwilling to risk a rebuff. He'd come round to see me, he'd sought me out, that was true, but I'd taken the initiative, hadn't I? Written the note etc—and he hadn't given me his address until I asked for it. Even as I weighed up the pros and cons I knew very well I was only postponing it, I'd go anyway, in spite of all fears, shrinkings. It's not timidity, it's excess pride that makes you fear rejection.

The couple in the room next to mine were at it, I could hear them. Once I'd heard their voices, coming in, but they were faceless; I didn't know what their names were. All I was familiar with was the sound of their bed. It made a regular rhythm. I was so naïve that I heard it several nights running before realising what it was.

I made love to myself, stretched out full length on the monk's bed. The evening was stifling, a dull heat surged at the roof and I imitated it, threw off the sheets and let the soft slopes of my thighs entice each other. They were a couple, they clung to each other stickily, broke apart with a sucking sound. But it wasn't enough, I wanted them to burst into blossom. I got a towel and knotted my legs together, hid my sex, achieved the constriction of an embrace. My body writhed slowly like a woman, I looked down at the floor through the glistening hairs of my armpit, let out low moans like a prostitute struggling to earn her money. I shut my eyes so that my hands could go over me like lovers. The couple strained, swelled against the knot and it parted, my erection rammed the door and shook the wall, it was gigantic. Sperm shot up to the ceiling and cascaded, spattered my chest, smeared my groin. I decayed, lay stagnant, held my breath.

Somebody was banging on the door along the landing, where the couple lived. That was the noise I'd heard. They hammered again, once, then I heard the footsteps move off stealthily and go down the stairs.

One night I opened my door and it was too much, ugly beyond words, an empty hole fit for crawling into and going to bed and that's all: nobody in their right mind would dream of sitting in it, not even to eat. I had to get out, it was either the streets or Lou Coltman. I knew I'd be sweating it out during the last few yards, plagued by all kinds of idiotic ifs and buts: well, that would come later. I sprang about with new zest, eager to leave, escape, giving my face a rinse, hair a quick comb through. I had a destination, a purpose, I was alive with expectation. Gave the room a rapid going-over, straightened the bed, washed out the bowl for cornflakes in the morning, emptied the slush of tea-leaves in the pot. Jacket on and I was ready, going. It was good to be going, great to have a reason for leaving, instead of having to flee as I usually did, pursued by furies, no directions. Went dropping down the stairs lightly and eagerly, feeling the jacket on my shoulders like a benediction, straightening my back inside it with a strange mixture of luxury and gratitude. Out in the street I patted my pockets to hear money and went prowling off for Slab Square, where the buses gathered.

It was Thursday, a warm sunless evening, the kind of summer evening you take absolutely for granted in a city in England; a heavy grey sky waiting in dejection over the Council House roof, and if there was any smoke rising it would be the same lifeless sky colour. The air warm and thick. On the bus trundling through the crowds—the open space of the square full and moving, a man in a dark suit up on the wall making a speech, his face congested, one or two on the benches listening, lots just walking past without giving him a glance—men were digging thick fingers into their collars and saying 'sticky'. A couple of hours earlier there had been a cool breeze blowing, so I'd pulled on a red cotton polo-neck sweatshirt over my shirt and now I realised my mistake. No wind now, I was too hot. I took off my jacket and nursed it, then dragged the bus window open. We roared over the canal by the Midland Station and I got up for the next stop. Still two stops away from where I wanted, but I'd walk from here. The conductor had given me rough directions. I was getting off too soon because I needed air, I told myself. I was sweating, but the fact was I needed time to calm down inside. This always happened: I gave myself time and I became worse instead of better. I blamed the red polo-neck, felt like a jockey in it. The street was grim, broken pavements, gaunt terraced houses stuck together, back-to-back and more facing, exactly alike and dwindling off in rows like railway lines. Windows bodged up with cardboard, a mongrel on a table in one front window scrabbling at the glass and going frantic with barking, mad bulging eyes following me as I went past.

Giving me the address Lou had said, 'Coming from town you'll see a cinema, the *Astoria*—we're not far past there on the left.' 'Who's we?' I'd thought vaguely. Now here it was, a scabby peeling little fleapit, two long cracked steps and then the paydesk, painted maroon and cream when it was built and never again by the state of it; more scars than paint. A crumbling temple, swallowed by the brick jungle.

A girl of fourteen or so with bared white face sat on the top step, keeled over sideways but awake, watching, gobbling me up with her eyes, with her whole face as I passed. Kid opposite mending the entrails of a motorbike in the gutter, spanner poised while he watched me by. It was like entering a village, the curiosity was intense.

All the houses had garden walls at the front, low humped barriers with a gap for a gateway, but no gardens: the tiny patch was scummy greenish concrete, a sump in the corner for the downpipe. I was nearly there, watching the numbers and more and more tense in my chest. An acrid smell from somewhere, perhaps a factory.

The air was motionless, nothing in the street stirred: it was so abandoned I could hear the youth tinkering with his motorbike, right back there by the picture house. I banged on the brown door and heard my blood beating. The houses seemed to press in, I felt watched.

No answer. Banged again, then heard feet clattering down bare stairs inside. Next thing, a fellow I'd never seen before stood in the doorway.

'Lou Coltman live here?'

'That's right.'

'First time I've been here . . .' I began to grin.

'Oh yeh.'

'Is Lou in?'

'No, afraid not. He might be back later, I dunno. He just went out.'

'Oh—well . . .'

We stood staring at each other, it was funny; a young bloke with a few days' stubble, washed-out, crumpled face, and very steady grey eyes, long-lashed. Suddenly I remembered something Lou had said that night in the pub—'You ought to meet Ron Cousins, painter. I'll fix it up one day.' I said: 'Are you Ron Cousins by any chance?'

'That's right,' he said, still not even the ghost of a smile, but his voice more interested, his face less blank. 'How d'you know that, mate?'

'Lou told me.'

'Go on?'

'He said I ought to meet you sometime.' I told him my name but it meant nothing.

'Better come in, yeh,' he said. 'If you want to, that is. Lou might be back—he sometimes comes in early. Sometimes not at all. All depends how the money is, all depends. Christ knows where he gets to. . . . This is his place, you know.'

'I know.'

I followed him in.

'I'm just staying here for a while. He lets me use his back room.'

'Oh.'

We tramped up to the first floor, the stairs painted blood red at the side and then bare white wood where there had once been stair carpet. Neat, narrow, industrial cottage stairs, not an inch wasted. There were doors opening off the landing, old panelled matchwood doors made flush with hardboard and painted yellow, with chrome numbers screwed on amateurishly. Instructions were pinned up on each door, a list of don'ts. No tea leaves down the sinks, no scum in the bath, no girls in the beds and so on.

Ron led me into number four and jerked his thumb at the notice. 'Look at that shit.'

'Friendly,' I said.

'Shitbags.'

My place didn't go in for those written litanies, you got it verbally at the beginning.

'Makes you feel at home,' I said.

'Yeh, well, it's cheaper than a welcome mat.'

'Suppose so.'

The room was small, with bare floorboards, old and shrunken, gappy wood, stained black so crudely that the stain was in daubs here and there all along the bright yellow skirting boards. The walls were white, painted over a pink stripey wallpaper, and again the job was slapdash, the stripes barely covered in places. The grate was blocked up with a piece of hardboard decorated by hand in a gay zigzag design like an African shield, black and white, the fireplace slopped over ineffectually with the same white stuff they'd used on the walls. Originally it was one of those modern brown tile abortions that squat like toads, millions of them there must be, spawned up and down the country in towns and villages alike. One wall, opposite the window, was pasted all over with newspaper cuttings: only it wasn't a wall, it was a partition, you just walked round the end and that was the sink and cooker. A kitchenette.

I don't know where it came from, it might have been curled up asleep under the rickety coffee table—up jumped a young, very virile Alsatian, wagging, ferocious wolfish teeth on show and great red tongue lolling out, planting its forefeet on my chest.

'Down, Sailor—down, yer great daft bugger!' Ron Cousins shouted, grabbed it by the collar and hauled it off me, then pointed to a chair in the corner and it slunk away under it obediently, a beautiful, powerful animal.

'Who's it belong to?' I said.

The dog was watching me, measuring and setting me like a bone, its soft melting gaze fixed on my face.

The fellow shrugged. 'Lou's I suppose—well it sort of goes with the place,' and he disappeared behind the partition.

'Want owt to eat?' he bawled, out of sight.

'Not me, thanks.'

'Tea?'

'Okay, thanks.'

I sat on a bed which was pushed against one wall and looked vacantly at a biggish painting hung above the fireplace, greys and blacks in subtle tones, a scrabble of lines as if inscribed in the paint with a pointed fingernail, nervy, fine like fusewire, some kind of dim bulky bowed figure emerging from the apparent mess of stains, blobs, bleedings. It was glum and looked drearily undefined, like something seen through a net curtain, but a certain gravity and struggling purposefulness saved it from mere sophistication, it glowered through to me, a bit aggressive and lonely. I found it disturbing, and began to wonder, to wake up.

'This your picture hanging up?' I called. Apart from the news cuttings, nothing else adorned the room.

'One on 'em,' he shouted back shortly.

He came out with a pot of tea and two mugs, let them thump down on the table, callous, and went back to fetch his food, a two-decker sandwich, pilchards smothered in mayonnaise in one layer, tomatoes in the other. It was huge, it looked as if half a brown loaf had gone into the making of it.

'How many sugars?' he said, and before I could answer, said, 'Help yourself.' I dug into the paper bag while he tipped the teapot over my thick green beaker and poured, letting the tea spout forth while he transferred his aim to his own mug. Tea ran steaming over the table, dripped on to his knees, scalding him, and he jerked back violently: 'You bastard!'

He sat on the other side of the table on a wobbly folding chair, facing me, frankly staring into my face and waiting, non-committal, as if he only had to sit there long enough and it would happen, he'd get the hang of me, find out what my game was. He wasn't bothered, but he suspected my motives. He had nothing to say but when he spoke he articulated very clearly, unlike Lou, who was inclined to mumble. This man liked to be what he was: he didn't see the necessity for hiding. I admired this, but it was so unlike my own nature that I withdrew into myself.

He lifted his tea like a tankard of beer. 'Cheers.'

'Cheers.'

He was still watchful and unwavering as he drank, then when it came to his sandwich he had to switch off from me, give it his full attention. He got it between his fists almost grimly, tomato slithering out from one edge. I laughed and said, 'You'll never make it, you'll get lockjaw.'

'Watch me,' he said, stretched his mouth violently and got a mouthful, filling up his cheeks. For a while he was unable to speak, so I sucked up the hot tea and waited. I felt curiously contented to be there, even though I wasn't exactly welcome. The man didn't pretend friendship, he watched and waited like the Alsatian, he was indifferent but he might be interested later. That was good enough. Secretly I was going to work on him, softening him. I began to like him, his resistance, and I was here, this was Lou's place. I was in, anyway. Here was a port of call, something different. Things might even happen here. It looked hopeful, I liked the feel of its free-and-easy atmosphere. I hadn't been in a room quite like this before, though I'm damned if I could have said what made it special. It wasn't special, that was the point. It was a transit place, a passing-through room. A test room. I began to feel pleased with myself, as if I'd already achieved something.

Still chewing laboriously, Cousins sat eyeing me. It was getting funny, I felt the urge to giggle. He wore an ex-army khaki shirt with one of the shoulder buttons missing, so that the shoulder strap dangled loose. His long fingernails were ringed with dirt, the fingers pale and surprisingly womanish.

'Good?' I said, to break the silence.

He merely nodded, chewing and keeping the deadpan look on his face, then said something I wasn't expecting at all, as if he'd suddenly made up his mind about me: 'You'll have to excuse me if I don't say much—I don't have much to do with folks. Keep out of the way. So I don't have a lot of practice.'

I nodded sympathetically. 'I'm not much better,' I said.

'Better?' he said, very quick, and again I was floundering. He was like he was for reasons of his own, aggressively. I hadn't meant to imply he was some sort of lame dog, or expect him to be touchy about it. So he wasn't completely out in the open, he could be stung. What the hell, I thought, he can be what he likes. But I quickly corrected myself with 'No, not better—I mean I'm similar.'

For reasons of my own I was out to please him. He seemed satisfied, but a little depressed, thoughtful.

'Good,' he said, nodding his head solemnly.

He startled me by beginning to whistle tunelessly between his teeth. It was aimless, like someone rattling coins in a pocket.

'Doesn't Lou have much company then?' I asked him.

'Christ yes, I'll say. Too bloody much. I push off out, or go into my own hovel and lock the door . . . thank Christ it's got a lock. He needs a lot of folk round him, Lou does, they come in bloody droves when it suits 'em. Drives you nuts.'

Suddenly it dawned on me how lucky I was, not having Lou here in the room. I nearly closed my eyes with pleasure of anticipation, visualising myself tapping secret sources of information, drawing close to the enigma. I hadn't understood either how much the enigma fascinated me. Lou the melter into crowds, Lou the charmer, the elusive seeker of others. Lou being friendly, Lou looking into the distance, through the wall, round the corner. I saw him once in a pub, helping a blind man to the door, steering him through the customers with great tenderness, with complete absorption, obliterating himself. Lou the saintly man. The nomad, diving into the streets to feel alone, to feel free. Lou who knew what was going on, the power, who had his finger on things.

'You say he likes people?'

'Christ knows if he does or not. He don't mind any road, he lets 'em all come. I can't complain, can I? That's what I'm doing here. He's a queer bloke, Lou is. I've got my own ideas on this coming and going he indulges in. Mind you, it's only my idea, I know fuck all about the bloke really.'

'Have you known him long?'

'Let's see, how long have I known him—two months? Not much more. Any road, he won't let on what he's up to, but my theory is that he's trying to get to know all kinds of people—as many types as possible. Know what I mean?'

I nodded, eager to keep him going.

'And not only types, he's out to collect experiences, anything at all. He wants to sit down in the middle of things and let it happen. That's what I reckon. I like old Lou but he's a funny close bugger, you won't get to the bottom of him in a hurry.'

'You're right there,' I said: thought of endless space, bottomless eyes, streets going on for ever.

'Ah, you think so, do you?' Cousins said, really alert and lively at last. He sat back and reached for the teapot. 'More splosh?'

I shook my head.

'What's he doing it for then?' I asked.

Cousins was filling up his beaker, he shrugged, the subject seemed without interest, beyond him suddenly. 'To find out . . . .' he said tonelessly.

'Yes, but when he finds out, what then?' I persisted.

'I think he might be on with a book or summat . . . I dunno. Ask him,' he said, rigid, unco-operative again, 'he won't tell you,' and he narrowed his eyes suspiciously, fishing a loose cigarette out of his shirt pocket and lighting it. Drawing on the cigarette he relaxed, the tension eased. 'You say Lou wanted you to meet me?' he said, brightening up, though puzzled.

'Yes he did.'

'An' now you 'ave,' he said heavily, mocking.

I grinned at him and he just sat there, stolid, not giving an inch. We had another period of complete silence, with him draining the dregs of his tea and banging down the beaker. Bump. The end of something. He was no longer my accomplice: the source had dried up. No vindictiveness in him: I guessed he was alone a lot and enjoyed making a clatter, maybe found it reassuring. Like his whistling.

'How's life with you then?' he said unexpectedly, and I took the hint. I'd been at the receiving end long enough, sponging it up, now it was my turn to flow. So I told him a bit about myself, glad of the chance to restore the balance. I was beginning to feel like some kind of snooper. He sat nodding, interested to know I was a stranger to the town like himself, who came from Leeds, then as soon as I stopped talking he jumped up, said, 'I'll have to leave you, I gotta meet this woman at the Ring o' Bells.' He made straight for the door, going just as he was. 'Come if you like,' he added, with a brusque movement of the head.

'I can come that direction anyway,' I said, wanting to hang on to my new contact for as long as possible. I felt obscurely dissatisfied, as if I'd made a poor impression. This was my last chance to impress myself on his memory.

Jolting into town on the bus I told him I was sure to run into him again before long, when I came out to see Lou.

He gave me a hard look. He had a flat spreading nose: from the side he reminded you of an eagle that was half monkey.

'Don't bank on it,' he said flatly. 'I live from day to day, me.'

We swung into the square and he dropped off the platform neatly as we swished round the corner, gave me the thumbs-up sign and was gone. It was only nine-thirty, plenty of people were strolling up and down, standing on corners. I stood where I was, fizzing pleasantly with my new impressions, not at bay or lonely for once. I felt alright, almost a stray citizen out on the town instead of a drifting, homeless wanderer. I stood leaning against the plate glass of a store, let my head go back and saw the night settling flat on the city like a slate, a grey-blue enormous cloud darkening while I watched, at the skyline some long ribbons and channels of amazing greenish light still running afire over the roofs as the sun died, killed by buildings. I stood wondering quietly what to do next: a new experience for me. Usually I went, my legs took me, I was driven.

# 18

DAVEY IN the street or from the vantage of a car was restlessly, voraciously on the look-out, eyes skinned for anything female; yet I wouldn't have called him a womaniser by any means. Let's say, not a philanderer. That conveys a cynicism, a calculating cold eye, a detachment and a readiness to exploit, to use as an object and then toss away. Pleasure object. Davey was innocent of all that. He wasn't guilty or innocent, he was simply unaware of the existence of that sly world. He gave blood, he gave heart, he tore at the innards of himself. Davey was consumed with hunger: he'd frequently say insulting things about women but he had to have them, his metabolism demanded it. His need for their response and sympathy was desperate and he could never satisfy this need: one woman was never enough. But with each one he'd be full of eagerness to give utterly, unconditionally, to the limit. This generosity was his great gift: I loved him when he turned it on me.

When I saw him in action for the first time, in the street, the market, shops, anywhere, and realised he was the most gregarious person I'd ever known, I wasn't so pleased. I grudged him his capacity to project his joy, his energy, flood his face with feelings, I was irritated again and again by his ceaseless sniffing for skirt, not so much indifferent to my reactions as unaware of them. But he wore no masks, no disguises, if he gave a girl the eye and she cut him dead, if he didn't even squeeze a self-conscious little smirk out of her, he'd mutter under his breath, 'Fuck you then, don't be friendly,' and on his face would be a genuinely puzzled expression: he'd frown and go quiet for a minute or two, really put off his stroke, hurt even. It sounds stupid and his face would look stupid, uncomprehending. How could people be like that? Wasn't he offering himself like a flower, like a fountain of charm, couldn't they see how he appreciated them, made them beautiful, snapped them up in a wink and loved every sweet morsel in his swinging glance, right to the curve of their instep? What was wrong with the world, what were they so suspicious about? He recovered in a few strides, in time for the next encounter. He was what he was, you had to accept him.

He professed love for me, more than once, his eyes soft and shining, and while he was saying it I know he believed it absolutely. It wasn't his insincerity I squirmed under, it was the knowledge I had of him by then, that I wished I didn't have. Of how indiscriminate he was in his friendships, how sinuous, how striding. Even then I drew back from judging him, preferring to take him as he was. I had that much wisdom. Who was I to say how many people he could love without it being a lie? If it came so easy to him, professing love, was it any less genuine than my painful, intensely given, one-at-a-time kind? I envied him his spontaneity, the free generous gush of him, while another part of me held back and distrusted it, always wanting to know what it was worth. I had to have relationships which meant something, but did that put mean limits on your life, your everyday impulses? It did for Davey: he was quite a theoriser when he got going, he took pleasure in spinning it out in words, the path he was taking. Politics, sex, society, it was all grist to his mill when the mood was on him. All you had to do to start him off was mention the word 'Tory'. 'Oh what shits they are, what mean little bastards . . . Can't they ever stop measuring life out in columns, profit and loss . . . the cunts! What did old Bevan call them, what was it? Vermin. That's it, he was dead right an' all. Keep the garden parties flying, keep quacking away with that stiff upper lip, and they will, oh my Christ yes, they'll rustle up funds in thousands of ways while those silly sods in the Labour Party sit round squabbling . . . and what the fucking hell, they're half Tory themselves. Don't get shut of the public schools, not yet, my Johnny ain't had a chance yet. Don't it make you spew. You know what, I reckon this whole fucking country is basically Tory if they tell the truth, scratch the working man today and there's a little shitbag Tory grovelling under his skin, itching for a mini-stately home, for clubs, privileges, superiority . . .'

He'd rant on and gradually shift gear and the vituperative yawp eased off into something less energetic, much more ambiguous and at the same time more vital to him, a definition of values, directions. Meanwhile I was using him to define myself, usually to my own dissatisfaction. I was tall as him but thinner, nervy, warier altogether: a bloody worrier. Davey would abandon himself to a black mood, bare his breast to it with a wild despair I found shocking. I ran upstairs once to his place and he was sitting on the floor of the kitchen, crying, a mess of eggs was spattered over one wall, dripping down in awful warning, like a diagram of fragmentation. Judy and he had had a fight, his boot had caught her in the side and now she'd gone: he'd go mad, stick his head in the bloody gas oven, he couldn't bear the pain of misery. He sat bunched on the floor tugging at his hair and rocking to and fro, sobbing.

'Let me get you a cup of tea, Davey, come on,' I said, coaxing him into a chair. I was horrified by his transformation, he seemed completely broken, finished.

'Oh God,' he moaned, 'what a thing to do . . . How did it happen?'

'She'll be back,' I said. 'It's happened before, hasn't it? Didn't you say it's happened before?'

'Oh Christ no, not like this, it was terrible. She ran out screaming, she was going to fetch a copper, she thought I was going to do her in. She needled me about this other girl, Linda, kept on digging and digging . . . I couldn't stand it, I grabbed a chair and ran at her, wanted to smash her to bits, anything to shut her up . . . The poor kid, you should have seen her face . . .'

'She'll be back, you'll see.'

He closed his eyes and his head fell forward.

'I'm a bloody madman,' he said.

He was in such a state I was scared to leave him, went off haunted by the scene, by his broken state. Next dinnertime I dived in to see if there were any developments and he met me on the stairs, smiling from ear to ear.

'Okay?' I said, baffled by the recovery, beginning to feel like an idiot.

'Eh?' he said. The question on his face was sincere. 'Oh that, oh yeah, we made it up. Come up here and have a dekko at these binoculars I sent away for, week's free trial and fifty years to pay, summat like that. Here y'are, me boy, peep through them lovely goggles at that view over the chimney pots. Bet you didn't think chimney pots looked like that, did yer?'

And Judy was there smiling secretly, unchanged, unmarked.

He was brought low by rows, tormented by ugly atmospheres, but he was never one to anticipate trouble. He lived from day to day, had no defences, but recovered rapidly if the woman was willing.

Gradually I saw that the differences between us were striking, and that what I was doing, as usual in my friendships, was effacing myself and playing to the other man, encouraging his dramatic flights, his flamboyant gestures, his wild speeches and comic turns. He was so fluid, changeable, furious, and I saw myself as static, stoically existing. He was impulsive, often disastrously so. Unless I was driven, I always knew what I was going to do, well before I did it. Davey was either brimming over with self-confidence, full of bounce and resolution, his impetus taking him headlong over obstacles I would have baulked at, or he was absurdly bashful and blushing. My trouble was shyness, a very different disease. It meant I was continually unsure of myself, unable to assert myself, bitterly uncertain of other people's opinions of me. Half the time I was too withdrawn to be noticed, I felt. Friends tended to dominate, call the tune, because of my initial self-effacing trait, and a streak of cowardice in me made me avoid rows whenever possible. If I got sick of the domineering side of someone, if it didn't suit me to agree, I could call on some stubbornness and very rarely I'd let fly, stand my ground and insist on doing what *I* wanted for a change. But if it meant a scene I preferred to compromise, even though I'd accuse myself afterwards of being gutless. Having a row always boomeranged on me: I'd brood on it for days, re-enact it, reopen all the wounds. In short, we were both emotional flounderers, we lived emotionally, yet looking at Davey I despised myself for being secretive instead of suicidally in the open and hand-to-mouth like him.

The point was, he took no account of others. He was sensitive, yet curiously unaware, oblivious. If he was grief-stricken he howled, whether there was company in the room or not; and flowing over with joy he had to share it, no matter how little it mattered to the sharer. He ignored all the evidence. I could never be like that, but I admired him. And loved his power to seize on moments of happiness, suck the marrow of a moment just as a child does, without the slightest self-consciousness.

'I tell you what,' he said once, jogging along beside me in the street one dinner hour—I was on the way back to work and he'd taken it into his head to come and look at the dump I spent my days in. There it was facing us, four storeys of the usual box, concrete and glass and forlorn coloured plastic panels, around the base a litter of cars, vans, Land-Rovers. Davey forgot what he was going to tell me; his mouth fell open.

'So long then,' I said, suddenly embarrassed by his

presence, resenting him there as a gawping witness to my incarceration. I wanted to scuttle inside anonymously with the other work slaves. But he was standing still with his head back and his mouth open as if he'd seen a vision.

'Oh Colin you poor fucker,' he said, really aghast.

Instead of being angry I was touched, and I laughed, it was so funny. I came back to him and said, 'Look, I'm not the only one, am I? There's hundreds of us altogether.'

He was sighing, shaking his head as he turned away; then he remembered something important and his face lit up.

'I tell you what,' he said happily. 'Tomorrow's Saturday, what about us going up Dovedale way and sleeping out? We'll take a tent but if it's dry we'll just kip on the ground, lie on our backs and count stars like sheep. Ever slept in the open, have you?'

'No, never.'

'That's what we'll do then!' His face shone, he looked astounded, as if the idea had hit him with the force of a wave, washing him into paradise. 'Bugger me, I'm so looking forward to it—get us purged of all this shit. Won't it be great, eh? You know, you can lie there in the middle of it and forget clean about the traffic knifing across from one city to the next, racing each other's knackers off as if the gate's going to clang shut on 'em and they'll be locked out of all them lovely shitty streets . . . You lie on your back scratching your balls and right overhead is a lark bubbling away and that's all, splintering out its song fit to bust, faint and strong and steady. It's virgin out there, Colin, honest, the purity is fantastic. And silent! Yet you know it's teeming with life. I lay out there once all day on me belly, hid meself away and watched. You won't believe this, but thirty foxes crossed over the tiny patch of the field I was watching. In one day, man!'

'See you tomorrow,' I said, edging away. 'I'm late, they're winding me in.'

'Ta-ra!' he shouted, broke into a run and went off round the corner like an athlete, like a thief.

Lou was urban in all his instincts, not against nature but unable to see its relevance. You got on a train and sat against the window with your paper, smoked your fags, went for a slash, found the buffet and bought a can of beer and if you noticed the country at all it was green, dun-coloured, farms and animals and old crumbly moss-covered walls and churches were part of it, stuck in the mud, stuck in the past. We'd gone on from that. It was there still, nobody had cleared it away, a few people pottered around there or went for visits at weekends, holidays, like they sat in their gardens or trimmed the grass on the graves at the cemetery. It was there but oh Christ it was boring, and full of nothing when they opened things up with some really new motorways. Granted it could be nice and peaceful and pretty but the point was, nothing was going on there any more. A void. In the cities was where it was happening, now and in the future: that's where the clues were to be found, in the streets. 'The Industrial Revolution happened here, in England, we were the first. Spread out from here, but you'd never think it. We still go round like yokels, we don't know how to act urban. That's why our cities are such bloody awful places: the people haven't moved into them yet. Anyway they're not fit. They're nineteenth century, we haven't got any twentieth-century cities. We've got a few new towns but they were born on drawing boards and can't you tell it when you step into one, what abortions.'

Whatever his visions of the new city were, the city he lived in he used like a vending machine. And the pub was his element; that was the place for human contact, his plaza. Davey, surprisingly for such a gregarious man, wasn't much for pubs at all. At night he wouldn't go near one, said he could smell the violence. He had a dread of the city at night altogether, the streets: he had a nose for hatred, for violence, perhaps because his own was never far below the surface. It was easy to enrage him, topple him into violence, especially if you were a woman and wanted to humiliate him. All you had to do was shut him out, cut off his supply of affection: he couldn't bear that. I was there once when Judy did it—I'd missed the previous instalment and came in when she was refusing to speak to him. I didn't know how long it had been going on, but Davey's face was white, tortured: I hadn't seen him like this before and he frightened me. The war of nerves went on as if I wasn't there, that was the horrible thing. She sat twisted away from him on the settee, sewing, mending a sock or something. Each time he bent over her shoulder to speak she snatched herself clear, turning her face away in a gesture of loathing.

'Judy, love . . .' he begged, croaking it, in a strangled little voice, his face drawn tight with the strain of struggling with his temper. But he was also in terror of being cut off, isolated, and the rage and fear mixed on his face. 'Don't be silly now love, listen, don't make a scene out of nothing . . .'

His voice crawled to be conciliatory, so abject I wanted to get up and kick him. All at once he grabbed her head in his long hands from behind and held it while he tried to kiss her.

'Get off me, you pig!' she hissed, breaking free and lashing out at him viciously with her arm. 'Don't come near me, keep off!'

She hurled her sewing at him and rushed into the kitchen, slammed the door.

Davey looked helplessly at me and tried to smile, but it crumbled. He let out a huge despairing sigh and sagged into a chair.

'I'm sorry, Col,' he mumbled by way of apology. 'She's so bloody stubborn when she gets an idea into her head . . . then I go mad and thump her one . . .'

'Perhaps I'd better shove off.'

'No, don't do that—hang on for Christ's sake,' and he gave me a wan smile, still sprawled exhaustedly in the armchair, legs splayed out. 'Things generally get more peaceful when you're around . . . we have to behave ourselves a bit. Though it didn't look much like it a couple of minutes ago, did it?'

He laughed shakily, a convalescent receiving a visitor, already on the mend. I couldn't help marvelling at him: in his shoes I'd have been laid low for the rest of the week after a scene like that.

We sat there. I kept him company for a few minutes. No words. The silence from the kitchen was hostile. I got up.

'I'll be going anyway, I think,' I said.

'Can't say I blame you,' he said.

'No, I've got to go,' I told him.

'Cup o' tea?' he said, without hope or enthusiasm.

'Tomorrow,' I said. 'Okay tomorrow?'

'You don't need to ask. You're always welcome, you know that,' he said. 'You're my best mate.'

# 19

SEE LOU again, he's important to me. See him before he disappears from view, before life swallows him up.

I was back again at Lou's place after a decent interval had elapsed. The street looked as mucky and forsaken as ever, yet less unfriendly. The door too seemed a trifle more inviting. Banged lustily, it opened at once and a nifty-looking youngster in cord jacket, a Paisley cravat, blue and emerald green in his red aertex sports shirt, stood looking mildly startled. He gleamed at the throat like a dragonfly. He smiled.

'Is Lou in?'

'Afraid he isn't,' the boy murmured.

'Ron Cousins?'

'Sorry, no.'

I scatched my head, baffled, was about to turn away and he added, 'I think Lou's only nipped in town for half an hour. Would you like to come up and wait?'

What manners, I thought, impressed in spite of myself. 'Alright,' I said, glad to be saved from defeat. On the stairs the boy said, 'I'm Steve, by the way.'

In the room I almost go to sit on the bed where I parked last time, then see it's occupied, a tousled blond head on the pillow, face buried. Longish hair, so for a moment I'm not sure if it's male or female. Hearing us come in he twists over, throws the sheets off to his waist and blinks up at us sleepily, raking over his bare hairless chest with one hand. He's older than Steve, my age perhaps.

'Hallo there,' he says, yawning. 'What time is it, Stevie?'

'Nearly eight,' says Steve, leafing through a magazine.

I can hear noises behind the partition, water pouring, crockery sounds.

'My God, isn't it dreadful,' says the young man in the bed, Graham, and to me he says coyly, 'We had a party last night, well an American poet visited us, friend of Lou's you see, and we celebrated with bottles of red wine, foul stuff, Spanish Burgundy wasn't it, Steve?'

'Don't ask me,' Steve says, 'I wasn't here.'

Graham laughs, gay fluttering charm of eyes and lips. 'No of course you weren't, aren't I stupid. Honestly I don't know who *was* here. Where on earth did they all come from?'

He throws back the sheets, he's in his trousers, his bare feet are narrow, elegant, sun-tanned. For a moment he sits admiring them, moving his toes, then swings his legs off the bed and stands, stretches his arms. I can count his ribs, he's a greyhound.

'Morning, Josephine!' he calls to the partition. 'Lovely evening! What are you doing?'

No answer. The washing-up sounds continue.

'Josephine?'

No answer.

He looks at Steve and shrugs. Tries once more.

'Josephine,' he appeals plaintively, like a girl, 'please tell me.'

'What's it sound like?' comes a woman's voice.

'Let me guess,' Graham says, cooing and malicious, holding up a shirt and examining it carefully around the collar, then suddenly turning on me the most charming smile, dazzling me with it deliberately. I've never seen charm used so flagrantly, with such deliberate intent.

The woman with the rough croaky voice comes out and I'm amazed, she's no more than a kid, white-faced and dopey-eyed, hair dyed a harsh copper colour. She's lifeless: she heads for the door without looking at any of us, and Graham says to her, 'Thanks for doing all that awful washing-up, love, you're a darling.'

He can't seem to open his mouth without sounding ironic.

'I didn't do it for you, I did it for Lou,' the girl says sullenly, not exactly resentful; just blank and sullen. 'Say ta-ra to him for me.'

'Why, where you off to, ducky?'

'Manchester.'

'Alright love. Take care of yourself.'

When she's gone I ask again when Lou is expected and Graham says without hesitation, contradicting his friend: 'You won't see him tonight.'

He takes a mirror from his hip pocket and props it on the mantelpiece, goes down on his haunches like a miner against a pub wall and combs his hair fastidiously.

'Steve, isn't it ghastly, I'm getting old,' he moans falsely, and a hard edge creeps into his voice. He glances over his shoulder at me. 'That girl who's just gone out, she's a pro,' he says coolly. 'I suppose you guessed, did you?'

'No I didn't.'

'Lou's been putting her up for a couple of nights. She's just had an abortion, she was in a bad way, poor kid.'

He's laying it on too thick, I think to myself, the coolness is exaggerated. Maybe it's my imagination but it seems that he wants to impress me, the newcomer, with their exciting goings-on. And it's true, as I find out later, that he is very proud of Lou. More than once he draws my attention to Lou's tolerance: even refers to it rather self-consciously as his 'humility'. His manner generally is inclined to be ikey, like a girl who isn't going to be had cheap a second time; he's a working-class lad and the genteel, mealy-mouthed accents are to elevate him in his own eyes. He doesn't despise crude men, he's no stranger to their backgrounds, but he fears their stolid living-rooms: he has to escape their uncompromising black-and-white realm. Ambiguity is his natural element. He adores Lou, emulates his touch of culture, and like any uneducated man talking posh he comes out with stiff, pompous phrases when he has something significant to say.

So he says, 'I can give you several instances of Lou's humility.'

Back to the present: I sit idle while Graham gets himself dressed to kill, flouncing to and fro looking for a tie, for socks, shoes. They're going across the city to Steve's house. Once again I'm stranded. All at once I remember the Alsatian, realise it's missing.

'Where's the dog?'

'Sailor? Lou must have taken him.'

'Is it his?'

Graham shrugged. 'Somebody left it here.' He glanced across at me. 'He's scared of that dog, you know.'

'That so?'

'Isn't he, Steve?'

But Steve is immersed in his magazine. 'Hmm?'

Graham laughs gaily. 'You should have been here the other night,' he cries to me. 'Sailor suddenly gets frisky, throws back his head and bays, doesn't he, Steve—charging up and down like a pony. Lou goes red in the face shouting at the thing, "Under the chair!"—"Down dog!"—"Sit!"—and pointing like this'—he twirls on heels like a bullfighter, to demonstrate.

Steve lowers the magazine to watch, amused. 'What does that prove?' he smiles.

'It doesn't prove anything, it was funny that's all. But Lou's scared of that animal. He is, you know.'

'Think so?'

'Yes and I'll tell you another thing,' Graham says. Not exactly excited, that would ruffle his composure, but speaking now with a certain authority, firmness: it seems out of character and I look harder at him. 'He likes being scared. Enjoys it. You watch him next time. That's why he's got the lolloping great hairy thing.'

'You mean instead of a smaller dog?' Steve says, a bit stupidly.

'That's what I think.'

Steve may look elegant, I think, but he finds it heavy going when he has to think. He is gazing fixedly at his friend in some perplexity, his expression a mixture of bewilderment and irritation. Really he doesn't want to be disturbed, he'd rather flick through his film star mag with his mind vacant, but now he's troubled. He frowns, he shifts on his chair, uneasy.

'I don't get you.'

Graham opens his mouth to answer, then remembers and swings on me, courteous in a mocking sort of way: 'I'm sure we must be boring you to death. I'm sorry, it's my fault, I go on so when I start, don't I, Steve——'

'No no,' I protest, laughing, 'if I can't manage to meet Lou, at least I can hear about him from somebody else. If you don't mind, that is,' I add needlessly.

'Oh nobody cares who hears what around here,' Graham says, flopping on the bed and picking a thread off his jacket. He's his superior self again. 'We love taking each other to pieces, it goes on all the time,' and he is using his normal, slightly satirical tone.

I begin to lose interest. But he hasn't quite finished being serious, he switches back to the subject of Lou's cowardice, which intrigues him, and he can see he's got me hooked and that delights him. He loves an audience. I try to make my face well and truly agog, to encourage him to pour revelations over me. Steve laughs out, 'Speak for yourself!' and I think, that's done it, but Graham has his story to tell, he's primed, nothing can throw him off his stroke. It flows out. Apparently Lou brings in one of his lame dogs one day—the expression 'lame dogs' means something important to Graham, he curls his tongue round it with deliberate emphasis—and the man is a real yob, a menace. 'He's destitute, Irish, he drools charm and he has this heartrending story to tell about his mother fished out of the canal all horrible, yellow and bloated. He looks the picture of misery, and Lou of course says he can doss with us. Well, he wanders off and I breathe again—how he stank! I've got a nasty feeling about this one somehow, but not Lou, oh no, he won't hear a word against him. Around midnight in he comes, blazing drunk, and starts smashing the place up. In the end I'm screaming at Lou to do something but he just sits there in the corner, dead white, trembling all over. The yob gets bored with breaking things and ripping up my shirts with a knife and makes for me, I rush out yelling blue murder, come back with a buddy, Big Jim, and by then he'd done over Lou, there he was with blood on his mouth and one eye closed up. He had an enormous shiner for weeks after, remember, Steve? But you know, do you think you could get him to kick this maniac out? Not Lou. "No, give him another week to find his feet," he said. "You must be mad, Lou," I said to him, "that mick's going to do you in, do us both in, if he stays here." He just shakes his head, that stubborn look on his face. And I can see he's terrified, yet he's made up his mind about something and he's got to go through with it. He's terrified, and at the same time he's getting a terrific kick out of the situation.'

Steve has been listening intently, leaning out of his chair. He pouts thoughtfully, working things out. He's thinking. Finally he settles back, opens his mag and flicks the pages as before: gives it up as a bad job. Graham sits where he is on the bed and muses, hands flat, fingers wriggling restlessly. In an entirely different voice he says, 'Steve, do I look respectable enough to meet your mother?'

And as if he's had an order, Steve jumps up. 'You know you look beautiful, you horrible man you.'

'Respectable I said, respectable!'

'Just right,' Steve says. 'Perfect.'

Graham is on his feet too, lounging in the doorway. 'You sure?' he says, and looks at me: 'I can't tell if he's joking or not.'

'Of course I'm sure,' Steve says. 'Come on.'

I go trailing down with them to their bus stop, unwilling to be on my own again so soon. Streets empty, blurring with the dusk of a soporific summer evening. We turn down a cobbled Lowry-like street of charred brick terraces mixed in with nineteenth-century lace factories, both sides, pitched steep on a hill, in front of each house a broken plinth of cement within a picket fence no more than a foot high, orange-box wood painted chocolate or bottle green or baby-shit yellow, uprights splintered or hanging loose like rotten teeth or ripped off for firewood, stains of rust from the nails weeping down. I don't know where I am, but it makes no odds, there's an endless supply of these mean streets. At the bottom of the hill we are on one of the big boulevards, traffic barging by in a steady procession. The bus stop is round the corner, opposite a modern pub throbbing all over with red neon, car park full at the side.

'Want to come with us?' Graham asks as we wait.

Naturally he assumes I'd like to, or I wouldn't be there. In a sense I would, but I mutter some excuse, standing between them both pointlessly, waiting impatiently now for them to depart: a queer tension has built up. A woman joins us at the stop, the bus roars up and then an extraordinary thing happens. Graham takes my hand softly, murmurs goodbye and before I know what's happening he bends his head in a graceful, feline movement and tenderly brushes my cheek with his lips. The next thing is comical but I'm stunned and too moved to laugh: the bus storms past, full up. I sneak a glance at the woman, who hasn't batted an eyelid, maybe hasn't even noticed, it happened so swiftly. Now we stand facing the empty road in silence, gazing blankly at the bloodily glowing pub. Without appearing to rake the distance I've spotted another bus coming, I don't want to get rid of them but simply put an end to the tension, which is much worse now—the crazy incident has given it an extra screw. The bus is stopping, I wait utterly passive now for whatever is going to happen, and sure enough he takes my hand again, I squeeze it to show he hasn't shocked me and encouraged he makes the same swift feline gesture as before, kissing my cheek. Steve smiles tenderly down, getting on, the bus gathers speed with a roar of triumph and I go drifting off full of strange sensations, deaths and births, touching my cheek with my fingers. Whatever I think of it later, when it happened the first time and astonished me I was suffused with pleasure, it broke down my isolation with beautiful simplicity, at one stroke, it seemed the most natural thing in the world. I walk in the vague direction of the town, a happy zombie, get lost several times, laugh aloud, going towards my grubby room because that's the direction my feet know, there's nowhere else they take me of their own accord. And for the first time in this city I don't feel alone.

## 20

I SEND Ray a report, making it sound more hectic than things are, putting plenty of swagger into it, as I always did when I wrote to him from afar. Off it would go and I imagined him opening it, his growing excitement, admiration, envy even at the thought of the life I was living, so untrammelled, and these new contacts, strange enigmatic characters I was getting to know. Opening his reply only confirmed my success: I'd be uneasy, guilty at once. Why couldn't I write him the plain facts? Nothing much was happening to me, was it? Not really. Yes and no.

What's going on up there, Colin?
Lots of things.
Such as?
If I told you, you'd never believe me.
Give me a clue.
How can I? That's the very thing that's missing.
I don't get you.
There's a key, but I keep losing it.
What?
Never mind—nothing.

If anything was happening I couldn't put my finger on it, the events I described were too nebulous to be interesting, so to avoid boring him I dramatised, seasoned things with significance. What I did catch was the busy roar of the city, such a difference to that timeless washing and pounding of the sea we heard day and night at the cottage, unfamiliar and maddening, insanely active I thought at first, until it sank away beyond my eardrums and I heard the steady pulse beat, old as creation, infinitely reassuring if you were in the right mood. Otherwise the most cruelly indifferent music in the world, worse than the squalling of babies. Life going on, howling, hammering at the doors. Reality roaring, in a fury of endless activity. Round the corner death waiting, eyes closed and its mouth open. But the thing I found truly frightening was the sight of that ocean coming at you in winter like a great grey toppling wall. I used to lie in bed in the dark and I could see it, it kept coming, if I didn't move quick it was going to bury me. I moved, I lived.

The curious unreality of my letters to Ray, except for the roaring sound and the feverish restlessness, both accidental effects, was I suppose matched by the vacancy of most of my days: I could almost say caused by them. The highlights were all I lived for in this city. Nothing in between was of the slightest consequence, I swooped down for the scraps, ardent, they weren't flung in my path very often and they had to mean something. I made them nourish me. If they quivered with light for Ray, it was me who gilded them. I was the morning sun, it was my moon that provided the madness. I couldn't distinguish any longer between the Lou Coltman I wanted and the one who existed in his own right. The same happened with Davey, he offered no resistance, he was made over in accordance with my need for kinship. I was threadbare, he clothed me. Both of them were unseeing, uncaring, deeply absorbed in themselves: my motives went unchallenged. Their needs were being met elsewhere. Aline was different—straight away she began to detach me from my image of her, I had to take account of her as a human being, separate from me. In my letters to Ray I said little about her because it was no good, she refused to fit into the dramas I liked to enact for him in writing. She resisted, simply by being herself, by making demands—and detached me too from the Lou and Davey I thought I knew. I began to see them in a new light.

A letter burning with impossible journeys came from Ray: 'If the lad would go off to sleep for four or five hours I'd have a go at a mammoth drawing, but he won't rest for long. So I dip into the sea off Sardinia till I can't stand it any longer. Every time I read it (Sea and Sardinia) this book makes me burn with envy and shiver with desire for those golden towns thrust up at the sky as the boat comes in off the sea, for the islands, the flower-opening sunsets and the brand of the sun above Africa. I grit my teeth and sweat a sea fever, an opalescent jewel melts in my mouth. I've had a taste of this fresh-created vivid world where the sea breathes in the cosmos and the land abideth for ever. I can never still the longing in my blood for what I drank in when I was a sailor-lad: not in voyage or ship but in the times of freedom between watches, on leaves. I'm no Vasco da Gama or even a potential Bilbo—one day I'm going to start a pilgrimage that will last as long as I live, an adventure in the living world amongst the things that fill the soul with strength and liberation. Now I dream of a voyage I made hundreds of years ago in a many-sailed schooner. There was no scurvy, no Captain Bligh, no purpose of cargo. I sailed with a knot of men who dreamed great dreams and lifted veils off the horizon every day. And for a long time we voyaged together and set foot in many new lands. We were full of simple joy. We knew the voyage would go on for as long as the earth lasted . . .

'I'm reading old newspapers to keep off the verdigris. There's a heap of them in a damp cupboard here. What I want is a really old one, say 10,000 B.C. Then I'd know who I am.

'Remind me to tell you of my nightmares one fine day. I am guilt personified. Sometimes I am struck with a club as I try to grasp where my old life, my relationships, my home life with brothers and mother and father all vanished to. The cut was utterly severe and I suffer for it, yet because what I want is so different from their way it couldn't be otherwise. It happened too soon, before I ever got to know my family. I struck out of the street and it's there behind me always like something I'm linked with forever and love and suffer for. If I'd deliberately planned to strike in the most vital places I couldn't have been more devastating.

'Outline of my life. Full stop. Now here's some curses, vows. I must have Change. Sod the stupid sheep, the imbecile docile cows, the scratching old hen. The way animals' lives are absolutely unchangeable makes me rage and quail. I demand it—CHANGE. Change, you silly bloody sheep, change into a ten-headed monstrosity but for Christ's sake change!

'I can smell the winter coming. I want like hell for us to get away and out of the rat-trap before much longer. England is a wonderful place, all it wants is a chance to die a natural death.'

## 21

IT WAS bound to be Lou of course who put me in touch with Davey. He was always the shy fixer: when he put two characters like Davey and me in touch he liked to fade away discreetly. It used to mystify me, how he could possibly get a kick out of such an introduction when he wasn't there himself to witness it, but I suppose it was the outcome he was more interested in. The grape-vine kept him in touch with that.

I never once saw them together. Davey was living out at Ilkeston when I first met him. He had three or four addresses in as many months after that, in and out of the city, and from what I could make out he'd lost touch with Lou altogether. Which didn't seem to bother him. Once or twice I tried to get him going on the subject of Lou, and immediately he'd be evasive, sullen, curiously resentful. Most ominous of all, he referred to him by his surname. 'He's a cagey bugger, Coltman,' he blurted out angrily one day when he was down in the mouth: he couldn't see where life was leading him except up the garden path, it had him by the balls (meaning Judy had) but by Christ he'd do something soon to change the pattern. 'I'm divided, that's my bastard trouble,' he said with soft bitterness, and thinking he was in the mood for self-examination I asked him what he thought of Lou—I seemed to go round asking everybody's opinion, trying to fit a picture together, intrigued—hoping it would lead on to the quarrel or whatever had brought about his present attitude. But that was his only comment. Whereas Lou had said of Davey, 'He's nice, you'll like him,' and I could tell he meant it. 'Don't be put off by what you might hear about him,' he added mysteriously. 'He's his own worst enemy, Davey is.' And it was working out the other way round: the one I kept hearing about from others was Lou.

They didn't have very much in common that I could see, only negatively. Neither of them had any time for the values most people accepted unthinkingly—and saying that immediately brought you up hard against their differences. Alright, so they belonged to a new post-war, post-Bomb breed: then you were in difficulties if you tried to embrace them both from where you were standing. Lou would never have used the word 'values'—there was a revolution going on, self-evident but we were all unaware of it, we needed to get tuned in. They faced different directions: if you thought of a bag of crisps ripped open in a city pub, the fingers heedless, the eyes elsewhere, that was Lou, and Davey slicing lovingly into a block of cheese and licking his chops appreciatively would be rural, harking back. Yet both children of the age, rubbed out and reborn on Hiroshima Day, fundamentally rootless, indifferent to tradition, no respect, no hope and no despair. Society was a load of lies round our necks. A breed free at last of the age-old cant—but there's your mam and dad still living, so unless you can be brutal you're only half born, half free, half out. Free and nowhere to go, nothing to do with it. Free to kick a tin can, free to piss your freedom up against the wall. What could you do on your own? Plenty, inferred Lou, the glint in his eye sent you wild to know, you hung on to him, he was on to something. Davey's bashing bitterness of his bad days was at least out in the open, naked, but unless you lived in Lou's pocket you wouldn't know how he was faring, good or bad. He was nocturnal like an alley cat, if he blazed or shrieked it would be at midnight. He was of the night, the city night.

A few weeks later this was literally true, his electricity was cut off for non-payment. The room was light enough while I was there but he had a candle stuck on a saucer on the coffee table, which had one leg falling off every time the dog rubbed against it. Ron Cousins had come in, grunted at me and sat on a cushion on the floor, leaning back against the wall with one leg doubled under him, morose and silent.

'All you need is a capful of money, you'd look like a pavement artist,' I said, to poke a spark of life from him.

'Oh ah,' he said tonelessly, shrugged, stared at the floor and that was that. I squatted on the bed nearby, looking down on the top of his head, the sight of his soft feathery hair correcting my first impression of him as a bristly uncouth lump of a bloke. I remembered his pale feminine hands from last time, looked again and saw I wasn't mistaken. But he had a hard, bitter rind to him.

Lou was looking distinctly twitchy; as soon as it began to get dark he wanted to be off, he needed the conviviality of a pub: but he was in good form, saying things like, 'It always amazes me how nice the English are.'

'They are?' I said, sounding dubious, yet in fact feeling pleased by such a preposterous statement. A good sign. Ron didn't even lift his head.

'I'm thinking of the electricity man coming the other day, eight in the morning, there he was with his bag of tools to cut off the supply. I was still in bed, I opened the door all bleary and this little ginger chap is gaping at me like he's seen a ghost. What a time to come banging on folk's doors, disgusting isn't it, he says, so apologetic, so friendly. And cutting off me electricity he keeps yapping away, nice weather we're having, live here long have you, he had a week at Skeg with the missus and kids in June and it never stopped raining . . . on he goes, while I bumble around pulling my pants on, and he apologises another five or six times before he's done.'

'I know what you mean,' I say, warming to him, grinning.

'Smashing, I thought. Worth getting cut off for that.'

'You'd recommend it then,' laughing.

'Ah, I would, any day.'

A bit later we adjourned to *The Iron Man*, leaving Ron

stubbornly miserable on the floor, had some good talk and I went off rejuvenated. Nothing had been said that amounted to much, but I felt in a current of life instead of stagnant and veering as I'd been before. So much so that I was totally unprepared for the next little development, swinging up the slope by St Peter's one Saturday afternoon, the town bustling with shoppers. Suddenly I had an urge to mooch about in the gloomy abandoned streets of the old Lace Market, obsolete towering buildings barricaded and empty at weekends. I went under the vast blocks of silence, it was like prowling through a museum. No traffic, you could walk on the cobbles in the middle of the road, peer up alleys, read the notices announcing the vacancies for machinists, stocking hands. At a high point a flight of steps leads down giddily towards the railway and a scabby black iron bridge, then more girder steps and a maze of little streets and a tea stall below your feet, just off the main road out to the Midland Station. I started down the first flight and met Ron Cousins, clumping up like a farm labourer in a field of mud.

'Seen Lou?' he said, and when I said no, I was thinking of going out tonight, he looked strangely crafty and triumphant.

'Out where?' he said.

'To the flat. Why?'

Then he comes out with it; the flat is no more, Lou's been evicted by his landlord.

'You mean the rent?' I asked, beginning to feel irritated by this character who insists on giving me the story in driblets, meanly. I can't understand either what's making him grin from ear to ear: he looks more cheerful than I've ever seen him. Has he got it in for Lou too, for some obscure reason of his own? And surely he's out on the street as well? What's so funny about that, for Christ's sake?

No, it's not the rent, he tells me. Lou always took care to keep that paid, bang up-to-date, whatever else went by the board. It was a rule with him.

'What was it then?' I burst out impatiently, more and more disliking the man's obvious elation, the air of furtive plotting, of secrets held back, traps being set.

At last I worm it out. Apparently the rot set in when the mad Irishman smashed up the room that night and did Lou over. The whole household was terrified, naturally, and when the rest of the tenants complained to the landlord they threw in everything else they could think of: weirdies coming and going at all hours, noise, pros, police visits——

'Police?' I said. This was a new one on me.

'That was my fault, an accident I had. They wanted details. All it was, I went up home and coming down again I climbed in the back of this lorry at a transport caff. Trouble was I nodded off, like, rolled out and hit the road, wham, travelling about fifty he was. Hell of a state I was in.'

'Where can I find Lou then?' I asked in a sudden panic.

Again the look of crafty pleasure flitted over his place. 'No idea, mate. He won't be gone far though. You'll knock into him, bound to.'

I did, and the upshot of it was that we decided to share a flat. We searched a few districts and found one on a hill, five minutes' walk from the hub of the city. Lou had to be near that hub. I couldn't believe the miraculous ease of it, or my luck. And with this golden opportunity to get to know Lou, fill in those missing details, came, almost immediately, the meeting with Aline, and so I was spending most of my free time with her. Everything happened at once.

## 22

IF ANYBODY had said I'd be having a bitter heart-searching row with Davey one day, all the more deadly for being half concealed, implied, conveyed by tone of voice rather than outright furious accusation, I'd have laughed in his face. We got on so well: there was nothing to quarrel about. We saw eye to eye on everything. Even now I can't imagine what it was about, can only think it was an explosion of resentments built up unawares over a long period, a steady accumulation of things we found irritating, disappointing, maddening in each other. That's the way a marriage backfires or a lovers' quarrel happens, so why not the row of two friends who think they know each other inside out and of course don't? It was a harrowing scene for me because the generosity between us was being smashed to pieces and we both had an urge to smash it; we sat motionless, festering, imprisoned in our cages of mean thoughts. Davey was talking a blinder, slowly working himself up into a frenzy and I couldn't understand him, the convoluted stuff poured out and it sounded pure gibberish, none of it made a grain of sense to me. All I knew, and I knew with absolute certainty, was that I was being got at in some unspeakably unjust fashion, and I trembled with hate for him. Both of us goaded to fury because we had nothing with which to accuse each other, yet the generosity we were jettisoning crackled and burned, reduced to ashes in seconds.

The memory of this scene weeks and months later would send me tracing back for signs, origins, like a man searching the ruins for some explanation of the disaster which brought his house down with such an incredible, inexplicable crash. Davey was living in a top flat, two rooms and a bit of a kitchen right under the roof at the rear, you had to ascend a twirl of steel steps to a platform hung in the open air, the door tucked under the eaves against the main chimney stack. He also had the use of the back garden, his steel staircase took root in one corner of it, among a clump of Michaelmas daisies.

I think it was while he was living there that I first woke up to the fact of how numerous his friends were. All kinds. Some real toughs, malingerers, students mad about jazz, like him, a photographer, young socialists and anarchists, an electrician's mate who was light-fingered—each time I dropped in there would be someone new. If he met a bloke hitch-hiking through the town with a bulging pack on his back, that was enough, a fatal attraction, he'd bring him in for a yarn and a night's kip, and more than likely he'd be hanging round up there a week later.

Frank Coggin was a good example: an art student on the loose from Newcastle, the spring term had started but not him. He wasn't going back. He stayed a month, would have been there for good if Davey hadn't winkled him out. He took root. 'He sat in that chair nursing a sketchbook, singing folk songs, wearing out my records, which was alright, fine, till he started getting demanding. "When are we going to eat?" he'd say, cool as you like. And never wash a pot, not a hand's turn with anything, the bugger. Would he, Judy?' But I knew how thick as thieves they both were when he first blew in; Davey delighted to have a real afficionado in the place, he dug out his records and they played them till one in the morning. They sat swopping yarns and singing songs and would have gone on all night. It was finally Judy who laid down the ultimatum, to Davey one night in bed. Either he goes or I do. He avoided decisions, there was no finality in his nature. Judy had found out long ago that decisions had to be imposed on him in such a way that his ancient cunning, his innocence, was helpless. He loathed scenes, his instinct was to turn his back and act sullen, boorish, if he actively disliked anybody; but Judy would occasionally force him into a direct confrontation by calling him a coward. It wasn't cowardice: to act meanly with someone he didn't hate was just impossible for him, a violation. I was with him once in a caff, we waited patiently for the usual dish-wash tea and pallid cakes. My cake was sawdust, topped with that ersatz animal fat cream, but we were hungry and it was eatable. On his cake the cream blob had gone rancid, he took one bite and dragged down his mouth. 'Take it back, get them to give you another one,' I urged him, but he wouldn't. He pushed it away sheepishly: 'I'm not bothered.' Sat looking at me a little uneasily, in case I jumped up on his behalf, until he couldn't stand the suspense any longer. 'Let's go,' he said, the second I'd finished.

Traits like this might irritate but they belonged to the good, positive side, like his indifference to money; they could never aggravate and boil up into a row. Did I begrudge him his guileless friendships with all and sundry, the spongers who battened on him, the deadweights who contributed nothing, was I jealous of that lot? No, I didn't think so. Anyway, I was never conscious of it. The more people I met who were connected with him, the more I felt our friendship was being slowly whittled away, diminished, and I had to admit the picture I'd first formed of him was changing too. As he was changing, growing, his paradise still green but a little tainted, his need for purity as infectious as ever but less urgent, his heart naked and soft when he shows it but he's learning caution at last, he doesn't bare it to fools quite so often. When he reminisces in a hoarse loving voice, low with wonder on the subject of childhood sweethearts, rapturous first loves and the shame of touching them, the urgency and guilt and sweet grassy flesh, and looming above it, arching over, his mother's steadfast heart, her tears, his father's clumsy, harsh word, shy pride, you understand how exactly his happiness is measured from his early days, a falling curve . . .

I used to see his motorbike parked outside at the front and that told me he was in. I nipped up the clanging steps and banged on the dirty window which looked into the galley-kitchen. The kitchen door was always open, I could press my nose on the glass and peer in to the living-room, right through to the street at the front. I'd make out a figure waving, either him or Judy, and let myself in. In those days he did a lot of swimming, going to the public baths every day when he finished work, ramping up and down for twenty, thirty lengths nonstop. He wasn't in a team or entering a competition, he swam for the sheer joy of it. He loved to try and explain in detail what it meant to him. 'I'm going to write songs about it one day, when I'm ready. I want to swim a few more years yet, then I might be able to. Colin, everything about it's great, there ain't nothing like it in this world, honest. I remember as a kid how exciting it was, getting your cosser and a towel from your mam, then paying your money, going in with butterflies in your belly and hearing the yells and echoes, that bloody awful chlorine smell getting nearer, marching round the edge gingerly and feeling such a nit in your clothes and boots. In the booth, that was great too, stripping off all nervous and butterflies again, like stage fright, that oilcloth curtain on rings you pulled across, the sweaty hairy bollocky man-smell the booth had, Christ it used to make me shake more than anything, that man-stink. Oh but the water washing over you, it gurgles past and you can plough away all day if you want to your heart's content, you're alone like a fish and nothing matters; I tell you you can't beat it . . .'

One night he'd just come in from his swim when I arrived, his hair damp and sleek, he was in the kitchen frying a couple of eggs and some bacon, a few left-over potatoes and beans for himself. He was happy, glistening with well-being: he had cracked his own record and lapped up forty lengths. 'What d'you think of that then, me ole sport?'

'You must be dead beat.'

'Shagged I am, fair shagged. Going up and down, though, it seemed so easy, I could have done a hundred, I reckon. It was only when I stopped I felt buggered. Funny, that. Climbing up the steps I was wobbling at the knees, then I caved in; had to sit down on my arse where I was for five minutes or I'd have fallen over backwards.'

I walked into the main room and a middle-aged, grey-haired man sat on a hard chair by the fireplace, a widower from down the street who came in sometimes. 'He's got interesting tales to tell, old Mac,' Davey had told me. 'Been to America, Australia, all over the place,' but whenever I was there he was utterly silent, sitting in his green pullover and collarless shirt, needing a shave usually, smiling his seraphic caved-in smile and observing the company slyly.

'Sit yourself down, boyo,' Davey called out in mock Irish. 'I'll be right widja!'

He sounded in fine fettle, I thought, settling on a stool on the other side of the grate. The evenings had turned chilly; I put my hands out to the fire, which had lumps of painted wood smouldering on it, giving off more stink than heat. Judy opened the door of the other room, poked her glossy, pert head in and said in the direction of the kitchen, ignoring me and Mac, 'I'm tired, I'm going to bed.'

Before Davey could answer she'd slammed the door. He came in holding the loaded frying pan, said, angry and defensive, to the blank door, 'You are, are you love? Good-o.'

He went back to the kitchen. I was used to these flurries, sat tight and maintained a stupid sort of neutrality, waiting for things to blow over, though I knew the chance of a gay evening was pretty remote when this happened so early. I I glanced over curiously at Mac to see his reaction. He was impassive, smiling thinly to himself and his eyes fixed tight on the smoke drifting up the chimney. I waited on edge to see what Davey would do, either try to placate her or plunge us deep into the gloom of his angry moodiness. This time it was neither. I heard a roar, something went smash in the kitchen, he yelled out, 'End of a perfect bleedin' day!' and charged through to the other room, the bedroom, eyes gleaming, murderous.

If he emerged again after a session like that and I was alone there, things went to a pattern. He'd have reached some kind of reconciliation, achieved a patched-up truce and want to talk wistfully, confide in someone, an ally, so that a warm intimacy would grow between us. I did my usual passive act, nodding and listening, dropping in the odd sympathetic remark—not calculatingly but because I couldn't help myself. And from this childishly injured mood of his would flow his confidences, then tender memories, hankerings and yearnings, the whole room awash with his happy sadness and I'd sit on the shore, dabbling my feet, uninvolved as ever yet drowsily enchanted by the gentle music. That's what he was, a musician, at such times he didn't need the record player, all he needed to do was play on the instrument of himself and reality dissolved. That was what was dangerous: he hadn't found a way to incorporate the reality behind the door; the clashing dissonances faded out and he'd have you almost believing they didn't exist, you'd dreamed it up, you'd imagined what was snarling and snapping nastily in front of your eyes. Everything was marvellous and blissful if you only shut your eyes and listened. 'If that silly cow would only let you,' he moaned. And another time, if you ventured to take sides, he'd cancel it all with some fanatical, unarguable statement such as, 'Judy means everything to me, if she ever left me for good I'd go raving mad, I would—I'd chuck myself under a bus.'

I suppose the deterioration between us set in during those visits to the roof flat, that rookery where they all congregated and he flapped his wings more and more impersonally. I became conscious anyway of something wrong, for a long time I couldn't put my finger on it. It was to do with the atmosphere, that was it. The kettle went on just the same, the welcome ritual, but I felt they were much closer now, in accord, and because of this closeness they were ganging up on me. I'd bang on the window, call out, get the answering wave and step into that kind of atmosphere which has voices hanging in it. I had the feeling they'd been talking about me, something derogatory. There was an air of insincerity, no more than a hint, but painful, hurtful. I was sure I wasn't mistaken—I have a nose for such things—but how can you ever be sure? And I wanted to be wrong. I must have wanted to, because when the storm broke, before I felt the surge of exultation which always heralds a release of home truths for me, I remember being astounded by the antagonism between us. I couldn't believe my ears. The sound of my own voice horrified me.

## 23

THE DAY comes, a Sunday, when I have to write Aline a note, simply asking if I can call and see her. We have had the little innocent tea-party, no arrangements made on parting, but somehow there isn't any need. Already, at one bound, we have reached an understanding. She's a book lover, an art lover; apart from that I know little about her, likes or dislikes, why her marriage is on the rocks, if it is, or anything. She knows even less about me. Strangers! It is that wonderful lack of knowledge I find so attractive, exciting, someone utterly devoid of credentials, brimming with a past and you're ignorant of it, but it has brought them in slow stages to your door, or you to theirs. So either you take them on trust as they are, just exactly as you see and sense them, that instant, or you don't, you reject, dislike, recoil. Either a spark leaps across the gulf or you're left stranded and unchanged; simple as that. So the spark jumps, we're connected, the separate boats we've been sailing untouched and so woebegone swirl together all at once with a life of their own. I descend behind her to the street, reach for the Yale lock and open it, swing back the door proudly, a master of life, like opening a casket, then move aside chaste as a priest with my head ducked while she passes through and out. And before the door closes we have exchanged rapt smiles and glances of absolute quiet willingness in the surge of the street.

'Can you come this Thursday afternoon, around three?' she writes by return. 'If you can, don't bother to reply—I'll expect you!'

Thursday's a work day but that's easy, I'll just be missing. I walk around at the depot with the measured policeman tread I've developed for killing time, spinning out the afternoon rambles, every so often pulling out the tiny note to read it again, though I'd committed it to heart hours ago. Afterwards I think how fateful are these first written words of hers, but taken in sequence it has the inevitability which things happening naturally always have, and you aren't in the least surprised or even impressed, it strikes you as being right; the only thing possible. We have arranged it all before, wordlessly, on the doorstep that evening. If the reply hadn't come —never mind the hosts of possibilities, the snags, chances of illness, sudden callers, acts of God, accidents, house on fire— that would have been incredible. It has to come.

I don't know how many unknown doors I've knocked on since I've been in this city. Lost count: all that matters, I say to myself, is that they've been leading me to this one—and the fits and starts of friendships have been priming me for this one desire. That's how it seems as the bus snores up and I read the words over the cabin, University Boulevard, climb in and ask for Queen Street, and now I do quiver like the bus window in my guts with fateful flutters, getting nearer, the engine driving me forward with the same grim grinding relentlessness it uses for delivering me at the gates of factories, offices; my heart pounds and goes sick and I think, Christ, is it all one process, isn't there any escape? Do all roads lead to the black rubber-tyred slugs carting you off to the cemetery, same deathly chugging beat, same blankly cunning attendants disguised as passengers? I glare, queerly scared, at the conductor wading up the gangway vague and unquestioning as a child. Jump off at Queen Street and begin to feel better at once, making my own way at my own pace to my own chosen destination, uncharted. With each step I shake free of the rigid engine-paced system, my trepidation is more human and natural, normal human-sized fears I can at least cope with. What does she think of me? Does she like me or have I imagined it, am I dreaming? Following the directions in her note I push on past the blackened brick terraces, dumpy and flush to the street. In the country they'd have been called cottages, straggling out and the dark hedges and flat fields starting: here they are all stuck together in a long dingy chain under one black slate roof, every now and then a sweet shop, newsagent, murky greengrocer's window no bigger than a house window, the sill mouldy with damp, falling to bits. Inside, skips of carrots, heaps of weary-looking cabbages, flopping cauliflowers, a woman standing at the counter with big forearms folded belligerently, pallid legs in ugly knots of varicose veins. I go by and she stops talking to the shopkeeper and takes note of me, granite-faced, arms knotted in a tight brawl over the frilly flowered pinafore. I can see a level crossing ahead and the hump of a brick bridge, then a great flat desert of ash and lorry ruts and rusty railway tracks running up to the beetling black fort of the power station plumed with white steam. I'm on the right road: march on grey and gritty inside, hanging on to meagre shreds of ragged belief in myself.

The disused, bomb-blasted look of the streets, the shattered landscape dominated by the power station block and its grid towers spanning the mounds of rubble, littered iron, battered car wrecks rusted out, gaping with jagged wounds all over, the smoking pits and black blotches of water, sinister as acid—my spirits sink at the sight of it and I have to stop myself running. What a plague-infested country. Like a fugitive I slink round the corner, the Godforsaken view mercifully blotted out and this is it, Chapel Terrace, a cleaner straggle of reddish brick houses, broken by an open space halfway down sprouting weedy coarse grass and defiant bushes, with unkempt branches snapped off by kids who have worn paths across the patch of green like cattle tracks, left a litter of toffee wrappers, ice cream papers, lollipop sticks.

Her house is next to this playground, a gate at the side into the back yard, since it's accessible, and the back entry to the rest of the terrace comes out here, the cindery mouth of it behind some bushes. No answer at the front, and I spot a face squinting down at me from the bedroom window of next door, over the entry arch. Being spied on unnerves me, so I decide I'll try the back way.

Before I can move, the door flies open.

'I was in the kitchen,' she says, glowingly beautiful in her summer dress, iridescent peacock colours, a scooped-out simple neck baring her throat, the skin faintly tawny from the summer sun on her throat and fresh cheeks and ripe round arms. In I tread, already bemused by her rich female gleam and glow, and this is the front room, her sanctuary as she tells me later. No hallway, opening straight on the street.

'All the houses in the street are like this, nothing between you and the pavement,' she explains, too happy to be bitter. 'I'm used to it, I don't care now. I hated it though at first.'

'Where I lived as a boy was like this, just the same,' I said quickly.

'Really?'

'Except for the contents—the decor.'

'Ah.'

And she glances round with pride, nodding, while I try again to take it all in, confused by this amazing room and the shock of coming into it from outside, the inferno view round the corner, one course of bricks keeping it at bay. It's late September. In cities I'm hardly aware of seasons, only time and temperatures, hot or cold, and whether it's raining or not: but this woman is. Because she is so aware, and I am her guest, I partake of her awareness. She is in touch with nature through the parks, her excursions, trips to the sea—within the last few weeks she's been to Skegness, to Ingolmells, and she speaks longingly of it and the cruel deprivation she feels in the city. Yet it is her city, she has favourite spots, Friar Lane, the Arboretum, the Forest, the Ropewalk, the limes of Wollaton: with her associations and her receptivity she gets more out of it than I ever could. And October, autumn—we're nearly there—is her favourite time, when the trees flame and the berries burn. 'What trees?' I want to say, ashamed, I feel exactly like a blind man, listening willingly but not intently, hearing the song she sings rather than the names, details of things.

The walls in the small jewel-box of a room are intense flat white, the skirtings and doors and window wood matt black; there's a long low studio couch in tasteful sooty grey, with other quiet touches of grey in hangings, cushions, bookshelves. Dove grey, silver stone. In a corner a standard lamp, heavy gold encrusted carvings on the pillar and big balancing lilac shade, the woman shimmering against the grey in her bold peacock colours.

Over the fireplace, in narrow gilt frames, two paintings: they are fantasies of decay and death in woods livid with tree trunks, clusters of spongy fungus, crimson and bitter yellow, nets of cobwebs hanging, festooning everything. They are rivers of dissolution. Then I notice a curious thing: the two pictures are complementary, the serpent writhe of them is like one circuit, it runs from wall to wall. Yes, they are her work but she's too modest to call herself an artist. So is her room her creation, and telling me in the low unsure melancholy voice she uses for involved explanations, her exuberant body such a contradiction, I can only think audaciously that she needs reassurance, I would love to reassure her. She is lost in spite of herself.

'They're a bit mad,' she says of the pictures, laughing, her eyes flaring in a kind of astonishment at herself, as if the things she does are always surprising her. Her delicately sensual lips smile at her own impulsiveness.

'There's mad and mad,' I murmur incoherently, inner eye still haunted by the vision of rape and pollution, clanking chains, the iron and sulphur progress-stink, presided over by that smoking fortress of power and its louring sky.

'Oh yes,' she says at once, warmly, gratefully.

I have the feeling she is replying to something personal I've said with my voice—by the sound, quite apart from the words.

She has a small cheery fire snapping—'It gets so damp in here'—and we consider the merits of the bluish tiled fireplace. 'I loathe the thing. If it was left to me I'd have it ripped out. A friend said he could build us a beauty, by hand, a stone one, but the landlord won't let us. Stupid man.'

I stand nodding foolishly in sympathy, saying at least it's bluish grey, not bad in the scheme of her room, thinking simultaneously that she said 'us'. Is she still living with her husband—was Marion right?

And I'm aware that although she is probably my age or only a year or two older, she is compared to me so poised, mature, dynamic in her body. Whenever she speaks I can hear the morbid sighing of her loneliness, the buried life that mourns in her, the bleakly sensitive mouth that her records unfreeze momentarily. These unshed tears are so poignant, they break something in me. But her melancholy is also sensuous, it slides dangerously like a snake, suave, self-destructive, or it can tread delicate and fluting and exquisite like a rain in the heart. She's a Debussy lover.

My laugh brightens her, joins forces with the lapping fire.

'I'm so glad you came,' she says.

'So am I.'

'Let me take your raincoat. We'll have something to drink soon. What would you like?'

'I don't mind. Anything liquid.'

She laughs.

'Aren't you easy to please!'

'Very.'

She is looking at me so steadfastly I have to lower my eyes.

'I forgot to offer you a cigarette—do you smoke?' she says.

And I shake my head.

'I do. Too many.'
'It's a matter of what you like.'
'Or can't help.'

She likes to express herself in innuendoes, but this doesn't satisfy for long. Sooner or later she has to be direct. She wants immediate answers. That's what her way of looking tells me.

'Come and look at these . . . but I'm afraid of boring you.'
'You won't do that.'

Out come her treasures for my eyes, and this is more than appreciation, I am being offered a whole interior life on trust. I don't know what to say: it's like one of her beautiful Japanese silk scroll paintings, you unroll it slowly, open little by little a world of ephemeral bamboo groves, a mere brushed-on suggestion of slender stalks, flicks and tints to convey the dry scratchy papery stems and leaves, swimming in a pale mist of moonlight at the side of the road; among the milky meadows parting stalks with their noses are the blurry foxes' heads, more and more distinct as the scroll unfolds. Bristling and still, pointed touches of ears and smudged skulls in the moonstruck bamboo groves like soft thistles everywhere: a crop of foxes.

Now at last I can contribute, air my knowledge. I gabble away about Hokusai, his life, the old man mad about drawing who lived with his daughter in absolute filth, had over ninety different addresses because each time the squalor overwhelmed them he simply moved, rented another hut. Utterly indifferent to money, he'd be paid for his prolific work and leave the packets of money scattered over his table. Tradesmen howling in with unpaid bills would be handed one of the packets: if they came back still complaining they'd be given an extra one. All he wanted was to be left in peace, if you could call it that, thousands of things clamouring in his eye to be drawn. I suddenly dry up, feel absurd.

'Go on,' she urges. 'Sounds fascinating.'
'That's all . . . I don't know any more.'

She is tearing open a fresh packet of cigarettes, Gauloises.
'You seem to know about painters.'
'No, not really.'
'Have you ever done any yourself?'
'I've tried, but I can't express myself properly.'

I look at her, overcome by an acute sensation of my clumsiness and ineptitude, my reddish hot hands, awkward stance. The fixed, porcelain beauty of her room confounds me, I swell red-hot, bubbling with a fierce lava of things I want to do, say. The room won't let me, disposing its elegant objects in a bland ripple of pride. The fire snaps, sends swift puffs up the chimney. I stand on the turkey carpet, glance down at my clumsy shoes, Aline in a deep chair by the bookshelves, drawing out a sumptuous art book with her slim connoisseur fingers.

She opens the pages, the heavy book sags over her thighs, I bend lower to bask in the alluring spread of a Van Gogh sunbaked land, smallholdings, woven fences, red carts with the shafts pointing into the sky. She is speaking and her voice breaks, a cry like a moan breaks from her; in awful clutching love we reach out and find each other, reaching across the fathomless gulf between strangers, her arm pulls me down wildly to her mouth and I drown there in the melting softness of her, tasting her sweet softness, filling my mouth with her hot breath, her frenzy, then the billowing soft sea of her body, warm and luscious and willing as it rises to her mouth and I taste it, my hand stroking down her side and over her thighs of its own accord.

Somehow she has got rid of the book in a sliding urgent movement. I take its place on her lap, we rock together in soft eruptions, closer and closer, rocking into each other as if we don't know what else to do, hugging ever tighter and closer with shuddering bear-hug convulsions. Literally I think I'm trying to frantically press myself through her skin to her heart, I want her heart beating inside me. How could I have ever been alone, how can I ever be alone again? In a sudden comical lull we draw back a fraction and become aware of our childish postures and it's alright, we rest on a pillow of peace and slow lust rising and the ripening concern of bodies, even our laughter sinks away, juicy and thick on our tongues, our eyes glossy and large with desire.

'Come down here,' she whispers, slips from the chair and we take to the carpet noiselessly like conspirators.

'Draw the curtains,' she tells me.

I jump up and make a false dusk, a dim dusty light. We roll into each other innocently for a moment, like campers, then freeze and lie still as stones, letting the firelight lap us, footsteps clumping by a few feet from us on the pavement outside.

'I thought they were walking straight in,' I mutter thickly.

At first she doesn't answer; she has her eyes closed, she is intent on her body's sensations.

'Yes, it sounds like that,' comes her voice, far off.

My heart beats in my throat, my tongue.

'You want me,' I whisper, iron-hard against her, prodding at her with a force that is totally beyond me, that surges up from the ground, from the centre of the earth, molten from the fire. It can split rocks, I feel, trembling, she'll be split in two, and to calm her I stroke her hair again and again, my mouth buried in her throat. I want to scald her, tear into her, and I long to comfort and heal, my chest aches with the intensity of my tenderness for her.

She clings to me powerfully; I go drowning down in her open flesh.

'Don't go away.'

She takes hold of me, opens her thighs, gives in and I swoop to and fro in a dream of unison with her, this unutterably soft bursten stranger wrapping me almost calmly, nursing me along comfortably in her big blossomy thighs.

We're weightless, the magic carpet wafts us clear out of the street.

'Darling,' she croons.

I want to laugh or giggle; it's so easy, life! Then the power begins to surge and take me, I lord it, I hear her hiss through her teeth and she bucks me, I go bearing down cruelly, burying the full shaft in her to the hilt. 'Farther in, I want it farther in,' she moans. That's what she wants, she snatches greedily, gobbling, she'd like to swallow me, balls and all, boots and all—for an instant I feel revulsion, I seem to hate her. Then her cries come, so pitiful, I am riven to the centre of my being, all my love comes spilling out in abandon for her.

'Take it!'

We lie on the shore of our passion, naked and shattered. The street still there, still outside, after all. The world eddying, circling; different. A sadness creeps over me for others, the loveless on the earth. I have sorrow for all kinds of poor devils; the sheer darkness of the planet oppresses me.

'Tell me what you're thinking,' she whispers, after what seems a very long time.

She is seeking reassurance, I think dimly.

'Thinking?' I echo.

It is a way of not answering. I begrudge having to speak, the crudity of it daunts me after the eloquence of the language of touch. I lag behind, regretful, I want to hibernate.

'You say so little,' she says softly, gently pleading.

Later she will say the same thing fiercely, challenging me to declare myself. But I have nothing to declare, can't understand her need. Being unfledged I think it's sufficient to be just blithely there. Words like 'Love', phrases like 'I love you' stick in my throat, I'll do anything to avoid saying them aloud.

'Do I?' I say, heart sinking.

The accusation has been made before, often, though admittedly in different circumstances. But it's the kind of remark that's liable to make me clam up completely. How do I explain that for me words are used, soiled, I grope in the void inside myself for words fresh and tender enough, and get lost. I want words that are like smells, where there can't be any mistake, like the smell of washed hair, the smell of newly-ironed clothes, the aroma of apples, pears, the swift wafting smell of flowers on the night air.

'Don't you like me?' she asks in a small timorous voice that's not really hers: I can't recognise her. She is at the mercy of her insecurity.

'No,' I say.

'I'm serious.'

'What a question!' I laugh, stupidly unaware of the danger I'm running.

I put my arms round her more tightly, hold her close, the fire gives a sudden sharp crack, a bit of coal exploding, and she jumps nervously; delightful. The slow hissing of the flames, the settling, shifting coals, sifting ash, we lie like babes in the wood listening. It's as if I've never really heard these sounds before: they've become part of our sensual happiness.

'Tell me about other women you've had.'

It sounds too ridiculous for words, I get a leering man-of-the-world picture of myself and I laugh. 'Had?'

'Well, you know ...'

'No, I don't. Tell me.'

'I mean ... made love to like this.'

'What makes you think there've been any?' I say, teasing gently, inwardly surprised and flattered. I begin to feel absurdly pleased with myself.

'Because you know what a woman likes. You know how to please a woman.'

'Oh.'

And her low appraising voice sends a shiver through me; like a hand curling round my balls. I begin to want her again.

'Won't you tell me who else?' she pleads pathetically.

'Let me think,' I say, laughing, enjoying myself.

Tempting, I think, to swagger out a story that sounds big, my path littered with abandoned wilting flowers: then it occurs to me that she's saying it to flatter, put confidence in me. Surely she can tell by my eagerness what a novice I am? As if to prove it, I do another perfectly naïve thing, trot out for her ears the whole story of Leila and what went wrong, why it could never have come right.

'Yes,' she murmurs from time to time, listening.

She listens with her wide clear eyes steady on my face, nodding and murmuring with perfect understanding, her longish, wide-apart breasts naked and vulnerable. A woman with bare breasts looks so defenceless, so at the mercy of a man. I finish, trail off into silence and she takes up another tale of frustration, an experience of her own, joining it to mine by way of illustration, as if it belonged there. These things are cyclical, she seems to be saying; I don't quite understand but her voice soothes and smoothes beautifully, even when she is describing pain and misery. I feel blissful, lulled on the sea of it. What I thought were bitter wounds begin to glow like medals.

Not a word though about her husband. I don't ask her, it doesn't seem to matter. Instead she says, 'I'll make you something to eat—something tasty!'

She jumps up and dresses quickly while I watch smiling, in the grey-toned room.

'Don't look, please,' she begs. 'Hide your eyes.'

'I want to look.'

'Well, don't.'

I study the fire, the slow smoke. The paintings.

'Now you can look.'

We both laugh.

'Dressing is a secret rite with me.'

'Why not?'

She looks at me, clothed, more sure of herself.

'What are you smiling at?' she asks.

'Just thoughts.'

'Tell me.'

'Oh . . .' I let it out slowly, in a long sigh of pleasure. 'Just that it's so barmy, so pathetic the way people go on, that's all.'

'Is it?'

'Don't you think so? I mean, everybody bunged up, constipated with problems, worries, anxieties . . . and there aren't any really, are there?'

'Not really,' she says, standing over me, shining. She doesn't agree or disagree, her smile is infinitely indulging.

'There bloody aren't any,' I repeat softly. The simplicity and naturalness of things suddenly comes home to me, astounding. What are we all struggling for, what are we bashing our brains out for, working and striving, trying to accumulate, to reach? It's here.

I stand before her, dressed, hands on her hips. She holds my waist lightly, there's a space between us.

'My ballerina,' she says, playfully. 'Sugar plum fairy.'

'With a wand.'

'Oh yes!' She becomes serious; she asks me calmly, her eyes full on me, 'You do like me, don't you?'

She doesn't flinch, she's hardened herself for the truth and intends to have it: she won't be put off. No compliments.

Arms around her, I say urgently, 'Can't you tell?'

She doesn't answer.

'Can't you?'

'I suppose I'm afraid of being hurt,' she said, with the faintest quiver of tears in her voice, 'I know it sounds silly . . .' and my nerves respond, shivering.

'No, no it doesn't.'

'I don't trust people very much. It's a bad habit of mine.

While I'm with them I do, then as soon as I'm alone again I start to doubt. That's horrible, isn't it?'

'I can understand it.'

'Can you?'

'You can trust me.'

'Yes, I think I can. I can't believe it, my trusting you.'

'Can't you?'

'I hope I don't stop trusting you when you've gone.'

'You won't. Anyway, I'm not going far. I can't, not now.'

'Oh I hope not. I want to love you terribly.' And she is clinging to me, kissing me. My heart breaks with love for her. It is going to be difficult after all, because of everything else. Painful, fighting in the teeth of all that's gone before. Of how things are.

I follow her into the narrow dark scullery, hovering near while she busies herself at the ugly blue-grey cooker, lighting the gas jets, working deftly, the blue rings of flame burning. Out through the narrow panes over the sink I can see the yard at the back, sunken, ground rising steeply behind, a shaggy bush on the handbreadth of waste ground to the side showing its head over the blackened run of brick wall. Path of bricks, sunk and broken, down to the dustbin, alongside the outdoor lavatory with its peeling green door, heavy downpipe painted the same standard green swelling down from the roof.

'Lovely view, isn't it?' comes her voice gaily, amused by my concentration. She detests her little prison-yard outlook, it sums up her isolation: she tells me this later. Now the ugliness can be skimmed off, skated over with child's eyes. Nothing penetrates the gaiety, the shabby world is created for pleasure.

'When I was a kid, there was a yard like this at the back,' I say. 'I was just trying to picture it. There must be thousands of backyards like this, all the same, yet every one different.'

'Now for some food,' she says, concentrating, scooping into her sizzling frying pan.

'Smells good.'

'Would you like to go in to the table?' she asks, oddly formal, and when I move to obey I take awkward steps. Sitting facing, plates before us, we're relaxed and happy again. I slice gratefully at the mushroom omelette, lightly cooked, browned on the outside. Lifting the cup of weak tea my hand shakes slightly, so I hold the cup cradled in both hands. I'm decrepit, I think, my excesses have aged me.

'Any good?' she says dubiously, watching me with the omelette.

'Good, very good. You're an expert.'

'You're distracting when I'm cooking. I want to look at you.'

'I'm a good influence.'

Her eyes narrow with laughter, and she contemplates, considers. 'Oh I hope so,' she says quietly.

# 24

NOVEMBER, gutters choked with gold leaves, red bonfires of leaves in the Arboretum: the autumn won't come to an end. I meet her outside the library, here she comes striding vigorously, pink-cheeked, opulent in furs; tucked under one arm her precious load of books, enough for a siege. Late November, winter sifting into the streets stealthily, in the night, under the cover of fog. Already there's been an icy flutter of sleet, like a chill brushing of wings.

She is comely in her shyness, offsetting this with the swinging arrogance of her walk.

'Now where?' I say.

We have a curious husband-and-wife familiarity. I seem to have known this woman all my life.

'Follow me!' she says brusquely, as a joke. But commands come natural to her. We hook hands and go off to the Arboretum, to inspect the Chinese ducks sailing the pond, near the cages where the peacocks live and the grotesque mina bird which makes human noises in a loud rasping voice when you least expect it. Then to a coffee shop just near the gates, a few yards from the convent school where she went as a girl.

'Are you angry?'

She shakes her head, she won't answer.

For half an hour we're the only customers: I can't believe it's a Saturday morning. At the small unsteady table she smokes Turkish cigarettes, grinding out the stubs in the ashtray obsessively, avoiding my eyes. Something is on her mind, I know the signs.

I am shut out, part of the tawdry everydayness.

'What's wrong?'

'Nothing at all,' she says in a bleak little voice. Usual answer. Lips thin with concentration, smiling unhappily at her own predicament. She sits back in a corner, a spider's stillness about her: a web of thoughts growing between her and me. I can't reach her, want to lash out at an enemy, I sit watching her bitter twisting movements as she grinds and grinds at her cigarette stub. I fight down an impulse to grab her wrist. She is pale, set, she knows she is being perverse. That's what her smile means. She torments me, but herself more. I clamp my teeth together, feel part of the city death, the hate simmering below the surface, I imagine cities with the lids torn off, bubbling with hatred underneath. The electric, grinding world bulges in, it's inside our blood. I want to spill blood, taste it. My eyes glare in my head, I feel yellow with venom.

She is smiling more naturally now, though still terribly tense.

'Don't worry,' she says, a little mockingly. 'I'm in a funny mood, that's all. I'm not nice today. It's nothing, really.'

She has changed, glazed and protected herself, moved away and hardened. She hides in a corner, smiling at me from a distance.

It comes out later that she distrusts me again, for no reason, nothing I've done. Afterwards she feels ashamed for doubting me. But I must say more, she tells me urgently, with real fear in her voice. I understand that my silences are making her suffer and it's a mystery to me why this should be. She has far too much pride to explain that she is plagued by an over-active imagination, undermined by a terrible insecurity. All she can bring herself to say is, 'Speak to me more often.'

Which brings her to Francis, her husband, a good, kind man horribly bound up in himself; a handsome, resourceful man whose only trouble is his Englishman's complaint. He'd rather fight a fire, enter a lion's cage than show some emotion in front of her, let alone talk about what goes on inside him—

self. If she makes any move that is likely to demand some emotional response he stiffens visibly: you can almost see him recoil, as if from something disgusting. He works at a firm manufacturing industrial chemicals, the new experimental wing out past the university—a great glass and concrete block, recently built and opened. She loves him but what can she do; their chronic lack of communication is killing the marriage. She blames herself as much as him.

'We're better apart,' she ends grimly. 'I feel I've got nobody, but he doesn't understand what I mean. I only make him unhappy, wanting him to be something he's not. That's it, really—he can't change. He'll never be any different.'

'Don't you see each other at all?'

'Oh yes, now and then. He doesn't want me to leave him, but I shall.'

'When do you meet?'

'At his mother's, every Sunday.'

'That must be jolly.'

'Don't be funny.'

'Well, I can imagine.'

'As a matter of fact, it's not that bad. Except that his mother blames me.'

'Naturally.'

'She doesn't say so. She doesn't need to.'

'Mothers don't, do they?'

And she laughs. Her sad laugh goes through me: all the forlornness of her predicament is in it.

'We seem to know about mothers,' she says.

# 25

'WHAT ARE you doing?' she said, stopping where she was on the other side of the room, half undressed, suspender belt dangling and her hands behind her back, high up, breasts pushed out as she undid the fastener of her bra.

'What d'you mean?' I said. I lay on the bed, watching.

'Nothing,' she said, and smiled her cat's smile.

I put my hands behind my head and lay there: I felt like yawning, but not my mouth; it was coming up from my knees, my legs, I opened my legs like a woman and the long yawn of desire came up from there, snaking through my blood lazily, circling up through my bones. I lay indolent and waiting with this weird endless yawn coiling through me. It was delicious, the soft moving lust. There was heat and grace and there was corruption in it, the flesh on my bones yielding as if it wanted to die.

'Don't watch me,' she said.

'Why not?'

'Don't, that's all,' she said sharply. 'You know I hate being looked at when I'm undressing.'

I closed my eyes, sighed, scratched my head. 'That's daft.'

'Never mind. Stop peeping.'

She came nearer, near enough and I pounced—'yaaarh!'—got her round her waist and bore down, toppling her on the bed. She gasped, laughed, starry and flushed. 'I knew, I knew you were going to do that.'

'When?'

'Oh, five minutes ago.'

'How did you?'

'I always do, it's just the way you start looking at me. I always know, I tell you.'

'I don't believe it,' I said softly, hoarsely, unwilling to grant her the knowledge of her power, though she had it and knew it and it was ridiculous to deny. Still, to say so aloud seemed too much, somehow it stuck in the throat. I held her and did nothing, moving my lips on her throat to speak, and without moving a muscle she absorbed me, my words, her enveloping softness drew me in.

'I can tell,' she said.

'No.'

'Yes. You have a peculiar expression on your face.'

Suddenly she clamped her legs together and caught me tight down there, like a naughty boy with his stick trapped. She kissed my mouth hard and her teeth bit down savagely on my bottom lip. Surprised, shocked by the pain I cried out into her mouth, muffled.

'Sorry.' She let me go. I drew my head away, bitten lip throbbing.

'What was that for?' I hissed, bitterly angry for the moment at her treachery, the betrayal. I lay inert beside her and felt the desire that had been short-circuited begin to run back, undulating. I lay still listening to my blood, its sing-song. Was that what she wanted? Was she out to punish?

'I'm sorry, darling,' she murmured, contrite and small-sounding.

'I don't get it,' I said sulkily, touching my bruised lip, wanting to draw out her remorse, force her into real guilt. I sucked in my breath between my teeth. 'Christ, it hurts.'

'I said I was sorry,' she said, the touch of impatience stinging me.

'Well, Christ, you're not playing the game.'

'Aren't I?' she said in a curious voice, sounding perverse.

I stroked her side, the long side curving to her back, I cupped my hand to the curve and stroked down the long soft warmth to the subtle swell of the hip, slipping behind, over the roll of buttock to the crack and down, behind the thigh to the shy knee-fold. She lay coldly, not stirring. I kept stroking, stroking, struggling not to hate.

It was dark now in the room and we lay in the bottom of the darkness hopelessly, as if in a pit. Outside the window the world pressed up, snouted, ugly, we were a replica of it.

'Men always have it over on you,' she said in a sour little voice.

'What men?'

'All the lot of you.'

'I'm the only one here, talk about me. What d'you mean, men? I wasn't stamped out on a men machine.'

'You don't understand.'

'Don't I?'

'Let's be quiet.'

'What's making you unhappy? Tell me.'

'Let's not talk about it. I'll get angry if you cross-examine me. It's not your fault . . .'

I turned my back on her. It was no good, a despair crept through my flesh. My face sank in the pillow: I had nothing for her.

'Now what?' she said loudly.

'Ask yourself.'

'Listen, Colin . . .'

'I'm listening. When are you going to say something?'

She moved away, avoiding me.

'Don't you want to?' she said, hard.

Into the pillow I said, 'I feel buggered.'

She came back, a mass of softness, tenderness, against my back, the backs of my legs.

'I know I'm a bitch,' she said softly.

She made love to my back, to melt me. She was intrigued, her arm sneaked around my waist, the slenderness excited her: like holding a girl, she liked to tell me.

'Aren't you smooth!' she crooned.

Her hand detached itself from the embrace, brushed down to where I was shrunken, wrinkled. The roll of flesh didn't unfurl under her dexterous fingers: she lost heart, fluttered briefly to my nipples.

'What a shame,' she mused. She was thinking aloud.

'What is? What are you on about?'

'That you haven't got breasts.'

I turned over flat on my belly on the bed.

She was fondling me, I must have fallen asleep. I was on my back.

'I want you, I want you . . .'

Then from lying there utterly congealed and dead it was changed to heat, to valleys unfolding, flesh in soft oyster clefts, in sticky furrows, and I didn't question a thing, let her sudden mad passion send me rocking into her hole. I filled her up slowly, vengefully, sank in hard to the root, quivering like an axe cleaving a log. Hearing her groan I began to lose control and worked helplessly, carried further and further down in the awful longing to unite, to marry, to decay and die, annihilate myself, burst out of the skin of myself. The flurry of cries unleashed a new violence and in the same instant melted the centre of me ineffably—that hard tight-lipped being who confronts the world crumbled into bliss, into tears. I was crying. I was a naked threshing weeping boy, the sobs torn one by one out of my chest and it was in the open, it was such a relief to be naked, stripped of vanity, frail as a shell. I'd forgotten how marvellous it could be. I lay like something foundered and lost forever, smashed to bits in the night, but it wasn't so, I mended, just waited on the waves of her breathing, swelling shape which took delight in nursing me back to health, and it came back slowly, a mysterious creeping stealth putting the heart back in my chest, the manhood between my legs, the clean bowels, strangest of all the wavering candle-flamey desire to live, very delicate and weak but there, smoking in my veins. And during all this time of strange mending she waited, endlessly patient and satisfied.

# 26

WE MAKE plans to leave. No prospects, we'll get on a train and go south, have a quick look round. I'll aim at Ray and Connie, make them my destination, they'll help us. I have a little money saved up. All I need to do is give a week's notice: Aline wants to pack a few personal things. The day draws near, we hardly refer to it. I write hurried notes to Ray, ask for copies of the local papers, to look for accommodation and some kind of job, but my heart's not in it, I'm merely going through the motions. The day of departure is all we live for, to cut free—and in a sense we're dreading it, for different reasons. She of course is fighting down her remorse in advance, also recurring waves of doubt concerning me, the strange young man she now has to trust. I'm an unknown quantity, and so quiet: what am I thinking, feeling? Why don't I say more? When she's with me she isn't sure of me, often she doubts me bitterly. Only when she goes away from me is she sure. Then she feels desperately abandoned, lost, she needs me.

I break the news to Lou: a hard thing to do because we've both turned out to be so secretive in our affairs. Living together has made him more furtive, elusive than ever. Most nights he disappears without a word, and when I come crawling to bed say at two in the morning, back from Aline, he's lying silent in bed, the other side of the room. Once though he wasn't asleep. I get undressed in the dark and climb between the sheets, aching all over, my nocturnal walks through the streets take me three-quarters of an hour and I have to be up at seven—and Lou mutters under the sheets lugubriously, 'You'll never live to be old, mate.'

Because he's such a bloody mystery and all that, I don't

see why I should bother to confide in him. But now I've got to. The chance comes one evening, we end up having a meal at the Silver Star, a restaurant off Parliament Street where we've been a few times, filling in till next day with egg and chips, beans on toast, big clonking stoneware cups of strong tea. Neither of us like strong tea in the flat, we drink it weak as piss, cup after cup, like Russians, but in the restaurant we just drink it as it comes, indifferent.

The bomb's dropped. No reaction. Has it gone off or not? Yes, he's heard alright.

'When you pushing off then?' he says vaguely, munching away. I can't believe he's so unaffected.

'Monday morning.'

He nods, then lifts his head with sudden decision. 'I'm having some more tea,' and he waves at the waitress.

Curious in spite of myself, I dig at him: 'Think it'll work?'

The waitress brings his tea, he pretends to be absorbed in her. He shrugs, spoons in his three sugars, stirs away with a clattering noise, vigorous, as if he's mixing a pot of paint.

'If you can cope with the complications,' he says.

'We'll cope,' I say stoutly, a bit untruthfully, no idea how or what, stiffened in defence against his jibing tone.

He lifts his head and asks bluntly, 'Is it what you want?' And I like him again, he's alright.

We eye each other, give and take, we're in touch for an instant.

'It is,' I say, with all the authority I can muster.

'Good, good,' he jibes lightly again. If he could talk through a yawn, that would convey his attitude exactly. 'Can't go wrong then, can you. Got to do it, haven't you.' He's not asking questions. 'Don't sit round asking people's opinions. What d'you want, approval? If you want to do a thing, then do it. Do it a hundred per cent. Don't arse about. Me, I'm going to drink this cup of tea. Okay?'

'Okay.' I laugh.

I like what he trots out, lean and flinty: all the same it's clear that basically he disapproves. He expresses himself too dogmatically, and that's not his style. He's angry. His idea of me has been knocked sideways all of a sudden. Well, I can't help that.

Two days before we set off I have a dream. Lou says laconically next morning, 'You were in a right state last night.'

'Daresay. Had a nightmare.'

Sitting in the train with her, the dream clings at the edge of my consciousness, hooks its claws into the wire of the cage and hangs there, weaker but clinging horribly. I can't touch it, can't kill it off, I have to wait for it to shrivel and die in my blood.

I am in a room I don't recognise, a dreary sitting-room at the back of a house somewhere, and there's a man in it, sitting lumpishly by the table. Blank, I sit at the other side of the room waiting for the man to speak, declare himself, but he doesn't seem able to see me.

It dawns on me that this is Francis. I've never set eyes on him before, have no idea what he looks like, but it's obviously him, sitting in a spotlessly white starched chemist's coat. He pulls a book from one of the white pockets, opens it meticulously at a marker, reaches in an inside breast pocket and brings out a pair of glasses. Sits reading primly, from time to time pushing his glasses back on his nose with the forefinger of his right hand. That's his only sign of life.

I bear witness to his every movement but he deliberately ignores my existence. I am being punished. I burn with shame, waiting to have my crime revealed to me. I find myself listening intently for his breathing, watching his chest for some movement. Nothing. Regular as clockwork his forefinger comes up to the bridge of his nose, touches his glasses. I wait for him to turn the page: then Aline enters the room.

The scene freezes. My heart beating, I sit watching while Francis stares at his wife. He fixes her with his eyes.

'Stop staring at me like that!' she bursts out irrationally.

He blinks nervously.

More calmly, she tells him, 'Take that silly coat off, for goodness sake—you're not at work now. I'll make you a cup of coffee.'

'I've had some, thank you,' Francis says, very stiff and comical. He puts his hand to his mouth, coughs discreetly, says in the same colourless voice, glaring blindly at her, 'in that café down by the market where we used to go, if we were shopping on Saturdays, remember?'

'Oh I don't know. Yes, I think so.'

'The old woman's still around, still there, hobbling in and out with those huge boots she wears. You know, the tramp. I didn't realise there were women tramps. Suppose there must be. Not much of a life, is it? Are they men's boots she wears, d'you think?'

'How should I know?' Aline almost shouts. She sounds on the brink of tears. She fears what he is going to say, to remember: I feel pain at her anxiety.

'Remember how she used to dress, that black shawl, and those great lace-up boots. My grandfather used to wear boots like that—when we were kids he took us with him to the cemetery, and he wore those kind of boots, with a loop hanging out at the back, to pull them on. They always remind me of cemeteries, boots like that, isn't it funny? That woman does . . .'

'I don't want to listen,' Aline says, almost imploring.

'Trudging along with her chin down on her chest—how could she see where she was going, d'you think?'

'I don't know!' Aline says, as if in pain. She holds her head.

'She used to drag an orange box over the pavement, on the end of a piece of rope. Bent right over, she'd be, dragging it, like those pictures of Chinese coolies on the banks of the Yangtse . . . Did she have her belongings in that box, would you say?'

'Oh shut up!' Aline yells, 'shut up, you damn fool, shut up!' And Francis closes his book with a snap, the noise resounds in the room like a gunshot. Aline looks very pale, drained, she wears no make-up. He stares into her face without speaking, ridiculously solemn, until I glance away in sheer embarrassment.

'I'd be grateful if you'd sit down a moment,' he says at last, his voice utterly flat.

Aline closes her eyes, then opens them.

'Why?' she says, surprised.

But she comes to the table obediently and sits facing him. Then comes a long pause of suspense. She waits with obvious nervousness, tensely expectant while he struggles blankly to speak.

'Go on then,' she says, gently now, her voice like a hand over his hair.

His face goes blank with inner effort, his throat working painfully. She gazes at him now with helpless pity, says, 'And take your coat off, you're at home now.'

Without glancing in my direction or raising his voice, he says, 'We can't talk with him there.'

'Talk about what?' Aline says. 'There's nothing to say.'

He refers to me in the third person: 'Can't he go somewhere else? I'll do something violent, I know I will, I can't stand the sight of him,' and his fists clench, he pleads with her like a child.

I choke to speak, heart pounding up into my mouth, I sit bound and gagged in the dream desperate to speak and can't force my jaws open. Aline puts her hands to her head in anguish, shouts madly, 'Leave me alone, I wish I'd never seen either of you!' and rushes out of the room.

For the first time Francis turns and looks at me, and speaking now with a queer shyness he says, in simple bewilderment, 'Where's she gone?'

I shake my head helplessly.

Forgetting myself, I go forward and sit in Aline's chair at the table, facing him: grip my hands together convulsively and lean closer, without any fear or animosity, to hear him whisper, 'Women take some understanding, don't they . . .'

The carriage rocked us, rushed us south faster and faster, the wheels howled joyfully over the points, we flew past the wayside halts and the whole land was in motion: cuttings rose and fell on either side of the train like brown waves. We dived into the sandstone hill, burrowed noisily in the dark, an onslaught of noise and fumes, hissing and hammering and frantic as though we were lost, emergency lights glowing weakly. We burst out against the sea and the light struck at us, the sky a faded December blue, lifeless above the seething thin shine of the salt water. The harsh smell came in at the window, the opera of gull cries lifted us clean out of our bodies. We smiled madly at each other, sea-mad glittering smiles pinned on our cheekbones. Nobody else in the compartment: we sat perched face to face, knees touching, holding hands, our faces reflections of each other.

Strange listening looks we have on our faces. I sit transfixed by hers and know mine is the same.

'Happy?' she says.

I nod dumbly, eloquent beyond words.

'Kiss me,' she says.

Kissing, my hand rests on her knee, slips between, caressing. She shuts her knees suddenly, tight as an oyster.

'I love you,' she says.

I kiss her, trembling, hoping she won't force me to speak. I don't want to say anything trite. Footsteps in the corridor, door slides.

'Ticket collector,' I tell her, tugging to get free.

'No!'

Just in time she lets go.

We hover along feebly at the edge of the sea, the water, light and air a free world of no dimensions. The train races with whirring dry wheels like a toy and gets nowhere. A soldier sways down the corridor, broad shoulders filling the space with coarse cloth.

Restored by the sea, the train plunges inland, lifting the fields and farms level with our heads. Now it has power, now it strides.

'Change at Newton Abbot,' says the ticket collector, a black bear of a man, confronting us. He backs out.

I pocket the punched tickets. 'What shall we change into?'

'Dragons,' she says.

We hold hands, the world of the sea releases us slowly, the train scents the town on the horizon, sends itself streaming into the curves. Hedges, fences, stone walls, the rubble of a high cutting stream past us. The world is flowing. The train masters us as it masters the landscape, includes us in its destiny. It can do it, it can do it, the wheels chant. Eyes of joy kindling, intoxicated, I lean forward into the adventure: anything is possible. My back is to the north but she faces it, blocked by me, my body. One day I'll wake up to the significance of that. Ray and Connie are ahead somewhere, not far, already living the new life with the odds against them.

December, end of the old year. The wheels abandon it: everything looks ready for a fresh start. You can smell change, something in the air. Green pastures scudding by, green, green. Sudden raspberry-red earth, Devon soil.

'There it is, look. Red.'

We sit like blades of sunlight, shining.